1000-YARD STARE

BY

G S WILLMOTT

Prologue

I read a story on the ABC online news website recently. I was horrified to think that someone who was helping others had lost everything.

We're all learning more about PTSD and its effect on our veterans and servicemen. Marc Webb a veteran of Afghanistan and suffering from PTSD opened up his house to other veterans dealing with this debilitating disease. The Webb family lost their house and cars to the bushfires, which ravished the Adelaide Hills in December 2019. I have recently completed writing a book about PTSD. After reading the Webb's plight I decided to donate 50% of the book's revenue to help the family.

By purchasing and reading *1000 Yard Stare* you will be helping the Webb family get back on their feet.

I contacted the ABC journalist, Shuba Ktishnan who put me in touch with Marc Webb.

My editor Sally Odgers offered her services free of charge.

Desma Pacitto my graphic designer also agreed to design the book cover at no charge.

Finally my distributor E-book Alchemy has also agreed to offer their services at no cost.

I hope readers will learn more about PTSD and contribute to those in need by purchasing this book.

Garry Willmott

CONTENTS

INTRODUCTION

Since time immemorial the 1000 yard stare i.e. PTSD has been documented in ancient literature.

The first known recording of PTSD was contained in *The Epic of Gilgamesh*. *The Epic of Gilgamesh* is one of the oldest written stories in existence. It is loosely based on the historical record of an actual Sumerian King named Gilgamesh, who ruled Uruk in 2700 BC. Gilgamesh's rule was so epic that his deeds inspired great myths and legends.

In *The Epic of Gilgamesh*, the main character Gilgamesh witnesses the death of his closest friend, Enkidu. Gilgamesh is tormented by the trauma of Enkidu's death, experiencing recurrent and intrusive recollections and nightmares related to the event. (PTSD)

During the battle of Marathon in 440-BC, Greek historian Herodotus describes how an Athenian named Epizelus was suddenly stricken with blindness after seeing his comrade killed in combat. This blindness, brought on by fright and not a physical wound, persisted over many years.

Other ancient works, such as those by Hippocrates, describe soldiers who experienced frightening battle dreams. Similar recurrent nightmares also show up in Icelandic literature, such as the *Gísli Súrsson Saga*.

Gísla saga Súrssonar is one of the sagas of Iceland.. It tells the story of Gísli, a tragic hero who must kill one of his brothers-in-law to avenge another brother-in-law. Gísli is outlawed and forced to stay on the run for thirteen years before he is finally hunted down and killed.

In the Indian epic poem *Ramayana*, composed around 2,500 years ago, the demon Marrich experiences PTSD-like symptoms, including hyper-arousal, reliving trauma, and avoidance behaviour.

Nostalgia

Over the past several hundred years, doctors have described PTSD-like illnesses, particularly in soldiers who experienced combat.

In the late 1600s, Swiss physician Dr Johannes Hofer coined the term "nostalgia" to describe Swiss soldiers who suffered from despair and homesickness, as well as classic PTSD symptoms like sleeplessness and anxiety. Around the same time, German, French and Spanish doctors described similar illnesses in their military patients.

In 1761, Austrian physician Josef Leopold Auenbrugger wrote about nostalgia in trauma-stricken soldiers in his book *Inventum Novum*. The soldiers, he reported, became listless and solitary, among other things, and efforts could do little to help them out of their torpor.

A Not So Civil War

Nostalgia "disease" reached American soil during the U.S. Civil War (1861–1865). In fact, nostalgia became a common medical diagnosis that spread throughout camps. Some military doctors viewed the illness as a sign of weakness and one that only affected men with a "feeble will"—and public ridicule was sometimes the recommended "cure" for nostalgia.

While nostalgia described changes in veterans from a psychological perspective, other models took a physiological approach.

After the Civil War, U.S. doctor Jacob Mendez Da Costa studied veterans and found that many of them suffered from certain physical issues unrelated to wounds, such as palpitations, constricted breathing, and other cardiovascular symptoms. These symptoms were thought to arise from an overstimulation of the heart's nervous system, and the condition became known as "soldier's heart," "irritable heart," or "Da Costa's syndrome."

SHELL SHOCK

Post-traumatic stress disorder was a major military problem during World War I, though it was known at the time as "shell shock."

The term itself first appeared in the medical journal *The Lancet* in Feb. 1915, some six months after the Great War began. Capt. Charles Myers of the Royal Army Medical Corps documented soldiers who experienced a range of severe symptoms—including anxiety, nightmares, tremor, and impaired sight and hearing—after being exposed to exploding shells on the battlefield. It appeared that the symptoms resulted from a kind of severe concussion to the nervous system (hence the name).

By the following year, however, medical and military authorities documented shell shock symptoms in soldiers who had been nowhere near exploding shells. These soldiers' conditions were considered neurasthenia—a type of nervous breakdown from war—but were still encompassed by "shell shock".

There were some 80,000 cases of shell shock in the British army alone by the end of the war. Soldiers often returned to the war zone after only a few days' rest, and those who were treated for longer periods of time sometimes underwent hydrotherapy or electrotherapy.

In World War II, British and American described traumatic responses to combat as "battle fatigue," "combat fatigue" and "combat stress reaction"—terms that reflected the belief that the conditions were related to long deployments. Up to half of military discharges during the war may have been related to combat exhaustion, according to the National Center for PTSD.

In 1952, the American Psychiatric Association (APA) added "gross stress reaction" to its first Diagnostic and Statistical Manual of Mental Disorders, or DSM-I. The diagnosis related to psychological issues stemming from traumatic events (including combat and disasters), though it assumed that the mental health issues were short-lived—if the problem lasted for more than six months, then it was thought that it had nothing to do with wartime service.

In the DSM-II, published in 1968, the APA removed the diagnosis but included "adjustment reaction to adult life," which did not efficiently capture PTSD-like symptoms. This removal meant that many veterans who suffered from such symptoms weren't able to receive the proper psychological help that they needed.

Drawing on research involving people who survived severely traumatic events, including war veterans, Holocaust survivors and sexual trauma victims, the APA included post-traumatic stress disorder in the DSM-III (1980). The diagnosis drew a clear distinction between traumatic events and other painful stressors, such as divorce, financial hardships and serious illnesses, which most individuals are able to cope with and which don't produce the same symptoms.

The diagnostic criteria for PTSD were revised in the DSM-IV (1994), and DSM-IV-TR (2000), and DSM-5 (2013) to reflect ongoing research. In the DSM-5, PTSD is no longer considered an anxiety disorder because it's sometimes associated other mood states (depression), as well as angry or reckless behaviour; it's now in a category called Trauma- and Stressor-Related Disorders.

It is estimated that 140,000,000 people in the world have PSTD.

Based on article in History.com

An Uncivil War

Chapter 1

Nostalgia, Shell Shock, Battle Fatigue, PTSD or Whatever You Want to Call It.

Causes of the American Civil War

It has long been assumed the Civil War occurred because the North was no longer willing to tolerate slavery as being part of the structure of U.S. society and that the political power brokers in Washington were planning to abolish slavery throughout the Union. Therefore, for most people, slavery is the fundamental issue in explaining the causes of the American Civil War.

It's not quite that simple. Slavery was a major issue but not the only factor in pushing America into a horrendous bloody conflict.

By April 1861 the slavery issue had been entwined with other major issues such as state rights, though what these rights were is unclear. The Southern States objected to the fact that the Federal Government was dictating what was wrong and what was right. They felt their whole way of life was changing for the worse and they didn't like it. The Southern States also didn't like the fact that, prior to the war, about 75% of the money to operate the Federal Government was derived from their area via an unfair sectional tariff on imported goods. The majority came from just four Southern States; Virginia, North Carolina, South Carolina and Georgia.

All these issues contributed to the American Civil War.

By 1860, America could not be seen as one society – the North and the South were like two separate countries, each with their own value systems and interpretation of the rule of law. It became North versus South, the Union versus the Confederates – and then WAR.

The Confederate States of America

South Carolina
Mississippi
Florida
Alabama
Georgia
Louisiana
Texas
Arkansas
North Carolina
Virginia
Tennessee

The Union States of America

California
Illinois
Iowa
Maine
Minnesota
New Hampshire
New Jersey
Oregon
Rhode Island
Wisconsin
Connecticut
Indiana
Kansas
Michigan
Nevada
New York
Ohio
Pennsylvania
Vermont

The South was agrarian; cotton and tobacco were the backbone of the region's economy with strong exports to markets in Western Europe.

The class structure in Britain was mimicked in the southern states. A local plantation owner was comparable to a lord and the local population within his territory were deferential towards him.

The South constituted a strictly Christian society that had wealthy men at the top while those underneath were expected and required to accept their social status. Social advancement for the less privileged was possible, but unusual. Invariably, one advanced within the senior families, the economic, political and legal brokers of their state.

Certainly, the wealth created by the plantation owners relied heavily on slave labour and this was accepted; after all, the first slaves arrived in Carolina in 1670. Therefore, the South regarded slavery as the natural way of doing things. If slave labour was no longer available to work the plantations, wealth of the landowners would have been seriously affected. It was not only the barons who would suffer, but also the local communities that relied on their support.

When the dogs of war began to howl in 1860-61, many in the South saw their very way of life being threatened. Part of that was slavery, but it was not the only part.

The North's way of life was diametrically opposed to the South; it had become an industrial powerhouse with an economy growing at an incredible pace.

In the North, you did not need to be born into a wealthy family; many poor boys, such as Samuel Colt who died a multi-millionaire, became entrepreneurs. Cornelius Vanderbilt was another example. Whether an immigrant from the Netherlands could have made his way into the social hierarchy of the South is highly unlikely.

The North was also a cosmopolitan mixture of nationalities and religions – far more so than the South. There can be little doubt that several important groups, such as the Quakers and other religious organisations in the North, were anti-slavery and wanted its abolition throughout the Union. However, there were also groups that were ambivalent and those who knew that the North's economic development was based not only on entrepreneurial skills but also on the input of poorly paid workers. While they had their freedom and were paid, their lifestyle was at best very harsh.

While the belligerents of the American Civil War were opposed in many areas, it became worse with the perception in the South that the North would try to impose its own values on their beloved land.

In 1832, South Carolina passed an act declaring Federal tariff legislation could not be enforced onto states. This meant that after February 1st 1833 the tariffs would not be recognised in South Carolina. This brought the rogue state into direct conflict with the Federal government in Washington DC.

Congress passed the 'Force Bill' enabling the President to use military force to bring any state into line with regards to implementing Federal law. On this occasion, the threat of military force worked. South Carolina capitulated.

It was at this time that slavery became entwined with state rights. The question was, how much power was held by a state compared to Federal authority? The key issue was whether slavery would be allowed to continue in the newly created States joining the Union.

This dispute escalated when the federal government purchased Kansas. The new state was officially opened for settlement in 1854, when both pro-slavery and anti-slavery settlers poured in at the same time, establishing a scenario of violence and acrimony.

South Carolina was the first state to secede from the Union, on December 20th 1860. It felt it was being dominated by a Federal Government, which was controlled by the North. Whether this was true or not is irrelevant as many South Carolinians felt it to be the case.

The secession of South Carolina pushed other southern states into doing the same.

With such a background of distrust between most southern states and the Government in Washington, it only needed one incident to set off a civil war and that occurred at Fort Sumter in April 1861.

Fort Sumter

On Friday April 12th, 1861 the attack on Fort Sumter by the Confederate army began. This event is considered the beginning of the American Civil War.

In 1860, a Federal grant of $80,000 was given to complete the construction of Fort Sumter near Charleston South Carolina, as it had lain unfinished for a number of years. The fort was constructed to hold a garrison of 650 men.

On April 12th 1861, General Beauregard of the Confederate forces attacked Fort Sumter. The fort housed three 10-inch guns placed to cover all the important angles. The fort also housed 8-inch columbiads 42lbs, 32lbs and 24lbs guns and some 8-inch sea howitzers. Fort Sumter had its own fresh water supply and a hospital.

All hell was about to break loose. More than 625,000 people would lose their lives, many of them children.

Union Columbiad

The fort was not fully manned when it was attacked, but it still held out until April 22nd after more than 40,000 shells had been fired at it.

By the end of the war in 1865, Fort Sumter was little more than a pile of rubble after constant shelling by Union forces.

UNION BOYS

V

CONFEDERATE BOYS

CHAPTER 2

Ohio 1861

James Imlay, or Jimmy as his family called him, was a normal, athletic thirteen-year-old boy. The youngest of eight, he lived with his mother, father and brothers. His two eldest brothers, David and John, had married girls from the South and were living in Georgia and South Carolina.

Jimmy's hometown of Yellow Springs, Ohio, was a pretty spa town, famous for its natural hot springs. Its history dated back over two hundred years. George Washington had commissioned a military hospital in the town after the revolutionary war.

Life was good for Jimmy. He attended the local school and had aspirations of becoming a teacher.

Ohio River 1861

Jimmy was aware of the rumblings of war, but like all his contemporaries, he hoped it wouldn't happen. His mother, Sarah, was more and more concerned about the tone of letters from her eldest boys, David and John. It was clear they both felt strongly about the freedom of the South and were willing to place their lives on the line to defend the Confederacy.

Robert Imlay, Jimmy's father, felt just as strongly about the abolition of slavery.

Brother against brother, father against son; war was about to begin within the Imlay family and across the breadth of America.

In Cincinnati and surrounding towns like Yellow Springs, hundreds of young men enlisted for military service; among them were Jimmy's brothers, Levi, George, William, Andrew, and Robert. Although their father, Robert Snr was forty-six, he also enlisted to fight for this cause he so strongly believed in.

The only occupants left in the family home were Sarah and Jimmy; it felt strange and very quiet.

The Imlay men all joined the Ohio 3rd Regiment – at least they would be able to keep a protective eye out for each other.

Robert Snr, due to his age and experience, was commissioned a Captain while the Levi was commissioned a Lieutenant. The younger boys were privates.

The first serious encounter the Imlay men had with the Confederates took place at Beaver Creek Dam. This was the first of a number of battles called the Seven Day Battle.

The campaign took place from June 25 to July 1, 1862, and featured six different battles along the Virginia Peninsula east of Richmond. The Union Army of the Potomac, led by Major General George B. McClellan, was over 100,000 men strong. Yet a new field commander, General Robert E. Lee, shifted this sizeable group of Confederates from the ultimate goal of Richmond and back to the James River.

General Robert E. Lee

The Confederate President Jefferson Davis had appointed General Lee as a military adviser, but when General Joseph E. Johnston was wounded during the Battle of Seven Pines, Davis asked Lee to take command of the army in the field. Lee immediately set the men to work building defensive positions around Richmond, leading his disgruntled soldiers to dub him "the Prince of Spades.'? Lee knew he could not protect the Confederate capital for long against such overwhelming odds. After General Thomas J. 'Stonewall' Jackson arrived with troops from the Shenandoah Valley Campaign, Lee prepared to strike McClellan's Union army.

McClellan struck first, sending two divisions of the III Corps to secure the Richmond & York River Railroad. The intense fighting on June 25 in the swamps around Oak Grove proved indecisive.

The next day, Lee took the initiative, assaulting Federal positions along Beaver Dam Creek, north of the Chickahominy River. The plan depended on a rapid movement by Jackson's weary troops, who arrived too late. Major General A. P. Hill's Confederate troops attacked as planned, but were beaten back. However, the Federals, with Jackson on their right flank and Hill and Lieutenant General James Longstreet to their front and left, fell back behind Boatswain Creek east of Gaines Mill.

The casualties on both sides were mounting up. One of the Union soldiers killed was Levi Imlay.

On June 27, the Confederates attacked in a series of costly charges. On the south side of the Chicahominy, a Confederate force from Major General "Prince John" Magruder's command attacked Federals at Garnett's Farm but were repulsed. The savage attacks convinced the cautious McClellan that he needed to give up his plan to capture Richmond and fall back along his line of supply.

The 28th saw little fighting except for a failed Confederate reconnaissance attempt at Golding's Farm. On June 29, Magruder struck the Union rear guard at Savage's Station but with little effect.

On the 30th, three Confederate divisions hit Union positions in a battle known as Glendale or Frayser's Farm. The Union division of Brigadier General George A. McCall was routed, and their commander was captured, but counterattacks stopped the Rebel advance. Farther north, an assault by Jackson stalled in White Oak Swamp, and to the south, Federal gunboats turned a half-hearted attempt by Major General T. H. Holmes back.

McClellan took up a strong defensive position on Malvern Hill a little north of the James River. Lee hammered the defenders with repeated assaults that cost the Confederate army five thousand six hundred men, but failed to take the position. Strategically, Lee had won. McClellan retreated down the peninsula. Richmond was saved.

Lee, whose reputation had previously suffered as a result of campaigns in Western Virginia over which he had little control, emerged as the Saviour of the South. By August, he had carried the fight back to Northern Virginia. The following month he would battle with McClellan again, this time along Antietam Creek outside Sharpsburg, Maryland.

Rebel Yell

Chapter 3

David Imlay managed a tobacco plantation, *Magnolia* for his father in-law Silas Veith. Employing five overseers and one hundred slaves, Veith produced some of the finest tobacco to come out of the South. David's views relating to slavery were diametrically opposed to those of his own father. This difference of opinion would ultimately lead to conflict in the true sense of the word.

The Veith family was regarded as one of the wealthiest in Georgia. Silas Veith commanded respect from both politicians and other plantation owners. Even the slaves under his ownership respected Silas as a fair and even-handed master. Generals such as Robert E. Lee counted Silas Veith as a friend.

Silas and his wife Annette were blessed with six daughters; Charlotte, Sarah, Emma, Sophie, Anna and Mary, and one son, Tom. The youngest child, Tom was only thirteen when war was declared between the North and South.

Silas and Annette were also proud grandparents to twenty grandchildren, all of whom regularly visited and enjoyed the vast grounds of their plantation, *Magnolia*.

When war began, all their daughters' husbands, including David Imlay, volunteered.

David had moved south from Yellow Springs, leaving Ohio when he was seventeen, looking for adventure in what seemed at the time a faraway place He worked on various cotton plantations before ending up at *Magnolia*. It was here, having worked his way up the plantation's hierarchy, that he met Emma Veith. After a two-year romance, the couple married and moved into one of the cottages on the *Magnolia* estate. David, albeit a northerner, soon adopted the philosophies of a southern gentleman – including the right to buy and sell slaves.

With the men of the family gone to war Silas was left with five overseers to run the plantation. Tom helped out after school and soon became a capable tobacco leaf classer.

Tom was as keen as his mother and sisters to hear news of the war and glorious battles against the Yankees. The young southerner dreamed of joining the fray and fighting alongside his southern brothers.

July 1863

Tom's birthday fell on the 4th of July. He would be turning fourteen.

His mother and sisters had organised a surprise birthday party. Their plan involved Tom returning from the tobacco-sorting shed to be surprised by his family and school friends waiting in the dining room. Tom normally arrived home at 4pm. Everybody waited in anticipation but when the clock struck 5pm his mother became very concerned and went up to Tom's bedroom to see if he had somehow slipped into the house unnoticed.

Her son wasn't there but an envelope addressed to her rested on his pillow. Annette Veith opened the envelope, read the letter and, beginning to cry, she collapsed on the bed. Eventually, the eldest daughter, Charlotte, came upstairs and found her distraught mother.

'What's wrong, Mother? Why are you so upset?'

Annette handed the letter to Charlotte.

Dear Mother,

I am sorry to tell you this way but I knew if I told you face to face you'd try and stop me.

I'm volunteering to fight with the Confederate Army. I know I'm doing the right thing for myself, my country and my family.

By the time you read this letter I'll be far away. I've changed my name so don't try and find me. With any luck I'll meet up with the boys.

I'm sorry I ruined my surprise party. (Yes I knew).

Say goodbye to my sisters and tell them I love them all.

Mother, I love you and would never want to hurt you, but I know I'm doing the right thing.

All my love

Tom

'I must let Father know. He'll be able to find Tom; he knows all the generals. Don't worry, we'll fetch him back,' Charlotte said.

'You read the letter, girl. He's changed his name. How on earth can we find him? There are probably hundreds if not thousands of young boys fighting.'

'Well there simply must be something we can do.'

Annette and Charlotte returned downstairs to the dining room and announced that the party had been cancelled as Tom had fallen ill. The last thing they wanted to do was announce Tom had run away to fight.

Silas Veith looked surprised. Tom had been perfectly well earlier that morning. Once all of Tom's friends had left, Silas approached his wife.

'Annette, what's going on? Tom seemed fine this morning.'

She passed Tom's letter to her husband, who read it and promptly slumped into his favourite armchair.

'You know we won't find him, don't you?'

'Yes, I'm afraid I do.'

'I can ask around, but I don't think it will do much good. They'll probably make him a drummer boy which won't necessarily keep him out of the firing line.'

The two distraught parents retired for the night, although neither slept very much.

March to the Beat of a Different Drum

Chapter 4

Tom's Portrait

Tom Veith made his way to Atlanta by foot and train, arriving in the southern capital late at night. Not knowing where to go, he found a safe place to sleep on a bench at the far end of the train platform. Finally, Tom nodded off, only to be rudely woken around dawn by a Confederate captain.

'What do you think you're doing, son? This is no place for a boy to be sleeping.'

'I'm sorry, sir, I didn't have anywhere else to go.'

'Well, from the way you're dressed you don't look like a homeless boy. What's your story, lad?'

'I've come to Atlanta to volunteer, sir.'

'Have you now? How old are you?'

'Eighteen, sir.'

'I don't think so, boy, you don't look any older than sixteen to me.'

'I've always looked younger than my age, sir.'

'I don't believe you son; however I admire your courage. Come with me and let's see if we can sort you out.'

Captain Norris led Tom out of the train station to a waiting carriage with a Confederate soldier at the reins. Once on board, the officer ordered they be taken to the main barracks.

Tom was in awe. There were soldiers in grey everywhere, horses pulling gun carriages, and rifles visible in wooden crates ready to be unloaded and allocated to newly recruited soldiers. It was a scene of frenetic activity.

Captain Norris guided Tom to the recruitment office where there were lines of young and not-so-young men waiting to be assessed.

Captain Norris approached the officer in charge and briefed him on his newfound recruit. The recruitment officer, ironically named Captain Grey, agreed to speak with the lad.

'Right boy, I believe you want to join the Confederate army?'

'Yes, sir.'

'How old are you?'

'Eighteen, sir.'

'Son, you and I both know you are not eighteen. I can either send you back to your parents or I can accept you as a drummer boy. The choice is yours.'

'I don't know how to play a drum, sir.'

'Don't worry, if we teach the older boys to shoot a rifle we can certainly teach you how to play a drum.'

'Well then, I'll join up as a drummer boy.'

'Excellent. Join the line for your medical and then we'll get you fitted out in uniform.'

Tom passed the medical immediately and was handed a uniform two sizes too large with a cap that covered his ears. True to Captain Grey's word, Tom was allocated a drum and taught to play it correctly.

A drummer boy's recollection of the various beats and rolls were considered instrumental in the success of any campaign. During the cacophony of battle, young Tom telegraphically communicated the officer's orders through his drum. He learned that one roll meant 'attack immediately' while another critical order was the drumroll instructing soldiers to retreat.

The most frightening roll for the enemy to hear was the long roll – the signal to attack along the entire front. The first drummer would begin alerting other drummers in earshot to also start playing the long roll. Eventually, all the drummers would be simultaneously playing the long roll beat; a loud frightening symphony of death for the enemy.

Tom quickly picked up drumming and the various connotations of the beat, and was soon ready to join the battle against the hated Yankees.

Yellow Springs Ohio (Union) July 1963 - Union

Jimmy Imlay was not enjoying being the only male in the household. He loved his mother very much and felt a sense of responsibility for her safety in such turbulent times. But, he also believed he should contribute to the war effort against the South. Jimmy was aware of several boys his age who had run away to join the Yankee army, and thought he really should do the same. He dreamed of finding his father and brothers, and fighting the southern rebels with his brothers in arms.

After this idea played on his mind for months, he finally decided to go. Late one night he wrote a letter to his mother and slipped out of the bedroom window. Jimmy headed south to Cincinnati and eventual glory.

Dear Mother,

Don't be angry, don't be sad. I've left to join the Union army and hope to fight beside Dad and the boys. I feel it is my duty as a man to do this. I'll write to you when I've settled into army life.

Your loving son,

Jimmy

Jimmy's First Drumming Lesson

Jimmy made his way to the main army barracks in Cincinnati and joined the line of volunteers ready to give their lives for the cause. When it was his turn to approach the large desk and two recruitment officers, he tried to look as straight and tall as possible.

'Name?'

'Jimmy Smith, sir.'

'Age?'

'Eighteen, sir.'

The officer looked up from his paperwork and began to chuckle.

'Eighteen, eh?'

'Yes sir, last birthday.'

'Really?'

'Yes, sir.'

'What do you think, Lieutenant? Do you think this boy is eighteen?'

'I'd say more like fifteen or sixteen, Captain.'

'Son, I think we all know you're not eighteen, not even seventeen, but we need lads like you in this army. We'll sign you up as a drummer boy and let's see where it leads you. All right?'

'Yes, sir; thank you, sir.'

Jimmy was soon fitted for a uniform and received extensive training on rolls, beats, and codes. After four weeks, he was assigned to the 4th Ohio Regiment.

His first taste of war would be at Chickamauga.

CHICKAMAUGA
LET THE DRUMMING BEGIN

CHAPTER 5

September 1863

The Battle of Chickamauga in Georgia saw General Braxton Bragg's army of Tennessee defeat a Union force commanded by General William Rosecrans.

Earlier in the month after Rosecrans' troops pushed the Confederates out of Chattanooga, Bragg had called for reinforcements and launched a counterattack on the banks of nearby Chickamauga Creek. After two days of battle and heavy losses on both sides, the Southern rebels forced Rosecrans' Union soldiers to retreat.

Bragg failed to take advantage of the victory, allowing the Federals to safely reach Chattanooga.

Ulysses S. Grant soon arrived with additional soldiers, and that November, the Federals reversed the results of Chickamauga and scored a victory in the region.

September 19th 1863

Jimmy was sitting on the damp ground, drum beside him, ready to go into battle. With him were five other drummer boys between twelve and seventeen years old. The early morning mist created an ethereal and haunting atmosphere, the calm before the firestorm of battle.

Chattanooga at Dawn

Captain Pierce approached them.

'Lads, we're close to engaging the enemy. Drums ready and follow me.'

The six nervous boys followed the captain to where General Rosecrans was assembling his troops. Thousands of Union soldiers stood in a formation stretching back farther than Jimmy could see.

The Rebels' drums could be heard in the distance – a haunting sound that drifted across the meadows.

They could just make out grey figures emerging from the mist, the beat of drumsticks on pigskin, and the sound of boots on the ground getting louder and louder.

General Bragg gave the order and the Confederates ran forward to confront the Blue Coats. Shots were fired, as was canon. Jimmy was ordered to drum the 'move forward' signal, setting the Federals in motion towards the Grey Coats.

The battle of Chickamauga had begun.

Jimmy and the other drummer boys were having trouble keeping up with their battalion. The pace was furious until the two armies confronted each other – a mere hundred yards separating them. Then, the dynamics changed.

Jimmy pounded the pigskin, giving his utmost to the drum so it would be heard over the gunfire and screaming. All around him, soldiers were falling. Others took their place; many of these toppled with horrendous wounds or were dead before they hit the ground.

General Rosecrans rode his white stallion up and down the Union lines, shouting orders to his troops. Smoke from the rifles and cannon fire created a thick haze, making it difficult for either side to determine who was winning this battle.

'Hey Jimmy, are you all right?' shouted his new pal, Billy.

'Bloody hell, Billy, I knew things would be bad, but this is crazy.'

'I'm not sure what we're meant to be drumming. I haven't seen an officer to instruct us for ages. Well, not one that's alive.'

Just then a Union captain rode up and yelled for the two boys to begin drumming the retreat roll. Banging their drums as loudly as possible, they heard the drums in the distance started up drumming the retreat roll in unison. The Federal army began its retreat to Chattanooga.

The Rebels weren't making it easy for the defeated Union soldiers, continuing to fire and running after the blue coats until the Union troops crossed the Tennessee River.

Jimmy was fording the river when a Confederate soldier fired his rifle. The Rebel wasn't aiming at a particular target, more of a 'don't come back now' shot at the retreating Federal troops.

Jimmy felt a burning pain between his shoulder blades. Falling into the river, he died; whether from gunshot wounds or drowning, it was not known. It didn't really matter whether it was a bullet or drowning that killed Jimmy. This young boy was another victim of man's inability to solve differences through negotiation rather than war.

Chattanooga: The Confederate Perspective

General Braxton Bragg decided not to pursue the Union army farther than the river and was widely criticised by his subordinate generals, including Longstreet and Forrest, for not finishing the job.

Though Longstreet and his fellow general, Forrest, encouraged pursuit of the enemy the following morning, Bragg was preoccupied with the toll taken on his army from the battle at Chickamauga. Ten Confederate generals had been killed or wounded. Overall Confederate casualties numbered close to 20,000. The Union suffered some 16,000 casualties, making the Battle of Chickamauga the costliest one in the war's western theatre.

Bragg's inaction turned a tactical triumph for the South into a strategic defeat, as Union forces were allowed to get safely to Chattanooga. Subsequently, the Confederates put that city under siege, but in October, General Ulysses S. Grant arrived with reinforcements, taking over Union command in the region. In November, Grant's forces reversed the results of Chickamauga with a decisive victory over the Confederates in the Battle of Chattanooga.

Young Tom the drummer boy survived the battle, and helped bury his dead comrades the following day. It was confronting for such a young boy to see such horrible carnage. He became introverted and suffered horrendous nightmares, reliving the battle. Although he was not officially diagnosed with nostalgia (PTSD) it was obvious the young drummer boy was suffering from the debilitating condition.

When the war finally ended, Tom returned home to his family's tobacco plantation. His father, Silas, had great hopes for Tom to manage the plantation but after a short while he knew his son would not be able to cope.

Whenever Tom heard a rifle shot, he collapsed on the ground, shivering. This was later called an anxiety attack.

Tom committed suicide on his 23rd birthday.

ABRAHAM LINCOLN

Four score and seven years ago our fathers brought forth on this continent a new nation, conceived in liberty, and dedicated to the proposition that all men are created equal.

Now we are engaged in a great civil war, testing whether that nation, or any nation so conceived and so dedicated, can long endure. We are met on a great battlefield of that war. We have come to dedicate a portion of that field, as a final resting place for those who here gave their lives that that nation might live. It is altogether fitting and proper that we should do this.

But, in a larger sense, we cannot dedicate, we cannot consecrate, we cannot hallow this ground. The brave men, living and dead, who struggled here, have consecrated it, far above our poor power to add or detract. The world will little note, nor long remember what we say here, but it can never forget what they did here. It is for us the living, rather, to be dedicated here to the unfinished work which they who fought here have thus far so nobly advanced. It is rather for us to be here dedicated to the great task remaining before us—that from these honoured dead we take increased devotion to that cause for which they gave the last full measure of devotion—that we here highly resolve that these dead shall not have died in vain—that this nation, under God, shall have a new birth of freedom—and that government of the people, by the people, for the people, shall not perish from the earth.

Abraham Lincoln – November 19, 1863.

NORTHCOTE

CHAPTER 6

December 1920
Northcote, Melbourne

The young man was sitting on a large wicker chair. Draped over his lap was a crochet blanket his mother had made for him. It was summer. The temperature was 90 degrees Fahrenheit. Yet this man wore a felt slouch hat and his khaki uniform as well as his prized blanket. His name was Harry Preston and he was formally a soldier of the Australian Imperial Force.

The screen door opened. Harry's mother, Martha, brought him a cup of tea and a freshly baked scone with jam and cream. She placed them on a small table next to his chair. He didn't thank his mother; in fact, Harry hadn't spoken at all since returning from the war. It was not that he had received an injury to his vocal cords, in fact, he had not been injured at all apart from a mild case of trench foot.

Harry was suffering from shell shock, which we now call PTSD.

Margaret, Harry's younger sister, opened the front gate. She had just returned from working at the Pelaco Company in Richmond. She was a seamstress and a highly valued employee.

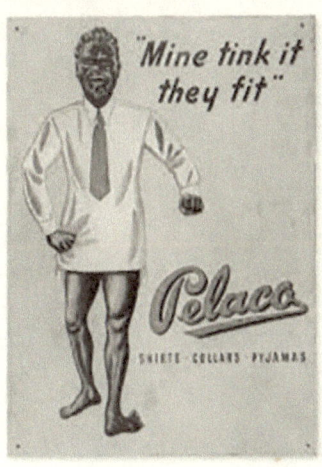

'Good afternoon, Harry, how was your day?'

Margaret was used to these one-sided conversations. She held out hope he would respond one day.

'I had a very good day, Harry. I received a pay rise. How about that?'

Harry showed no reaction. He just stared blankly straight ahead.

'I better go inside and help Mum with dinner. I'll see you at the dinner table.'

Margaret walked down the long dark hallway to the back of the house where the rudimentary kitchen was located.

'Hello Mum, can I help you peel the vegetables?'

'Hello darling, yes you could peel the potatoes for me if you like.'

'Sure, how was your day, Mum?'

'Nothing particularly exciting.'

'How was Harry?'

'Just the same. He just sits on the veranda, staring straight ahead.'

'I wish we could do something to help him.'

'We all do, darling. Oh, I forgot to tell you a letter arrived for you today. I put it in your room.'

'Thanks, Mum.'

Margaret went to her room to read the letter. She didn't receive mail very often.

She picked up the letter from her bedside table and examined the envelope. It had been posted from Sydney. She thought it strange, as she didn't know anyone from Sydney. She opened and began to read it.

1 December 1920

21 Dudley Street

Coogee

NSW

Dear Margaret,

You don't know me but I feel I know you very well. My name is Peter Bellamy. I was in the same Battalion as Harry. We were very close cobbers and fought side by side in a number of battles both at Gallipoli and on the Western Front. Harry used to tell me all about his family, particularly you.

Harry was a brave soldier who fought hard for his King and country. I don't know if you are aware he won a Military Medal during the Battle of Fromelles.

I am writing to inform you how Harry received his injury i.e. shell shock. It was during the Battle of Mouquet Farm near Pozieres.

Forgive me for any mistakes. I have not used a typewriter before.

Mouquet Farm

Harry and his four cobbers, me, George, Roy, and Bill, were in a large, reasonably dry shell hole trying to get some sleep in the main street of what was the village of Pozieres. Sleep deprivation was a soldier's second greatest enemy after the Krauts. The noise of artillery from the belligerents, the ubiquitous rats and lice all contributed to a bad night's sleep for your brother and us all.

Reveille sounded at 4.15am Harry kicked George who had slept through the bugle; George was the exception to the old rule. He could sleep if a shell exploded next to him.

We packed our gear and got ready to move on, they assembled us at the outskirts of Pozieres where the stench of dead bodies permeated the air.

Harry and the Boys at Mouquet Farm

We were marched about another two miles through destroyed terrain, heading for Mouquet Farm.

Fritz got wind of our approach and hailed us with shells. Many Diggers lost their lives in the first barrage. Harry and the band of four survived yet again; maybe Lady Luck was playing her part.

We reached our line but were told not to get too comfortable.

Harry's Battalion was ordered to move forward approximately two hundred and fifty yards and, secure a new position from there. Mouquet Farm was their objective.

Harry and his platoon were told to go over the top at 10.30pm.

The whistle was blown at 10.30pm on the dot. The Australian soldiers went over the top and ran towards their objective.

The Germans were expecting them. Artillery fire and machine gun fire wreaked havoc among the Diggers, many died that night.

The Australians finally took possession of the farm but at what cost? Three thousand five hundred young soldiers lost their lives in the first attack.

Harry and his mates were still together lying down among the rubble of what was once a beautiful farmhouse.

Mouquet Farm Before Battle

Mouquet Farm After Battle

I found a German soldier trying to hide. We decided we should put him to work digging our defence trench before his mad mates returned. Actually, it was Harry who leaped to his defence.

Margaret, I can tell you the young German soldier standing in front of us all looked terrified. He was sure we would shoot him then and there. I offered him a spade and the look of relief on his face was obvious. He began digging with great gusto, ensuring that we would keep him on our side. He didn't want to go back to the German front line. He'd much rather be a Prisoner of War and stay alive.

Just when we thought we might get some shuteye the German artillery started up again. It became a constant barrage for the remainder of the night. The casualty rate was climbing.

With the arrival of dawn, we could see what carnage had taken place overnight. There were dead bodies everywhere. Some had lost limbs. Others had lost their heads. It was like a slaughter yard.

Harry dragged out the German prisoner and assembled the other blokes and started to bury the slain as best they could. Covered, the rats couldn't get to them.

We had no food and all of us were starving. We all began to complain.

'Well, I think the bad news is we're not gunna get food anytime soon.' Harry claimed.

Just then, the German artillery started up again. We could now see the enemy's position. Their shells were starting to find their mark. Our appetites suddenly disappeared.

Major Jeffries, our commanding officer, ordered some men to escort the wounded and any German prisoners they had captured to the rear where the dressing stations were located. The prisoners were marched off to where a POW camp had been established near Amiens.

Orders came through for the 59th Battalion to move off to the left eleven hundred yards.

Aerial View Before and After Mouquet Farm

August 14

The rain bucketed down all night, making the trenches a muddy bog, and the incessant rain continued on into the day. There was a good reason why we all called it Mucky Farm.

'I suppose there's one thing going in our favour... the Boche haven't started up again with their bloody big guns,' said George.

'No, it's been a little quiet of late. I wonder what the bastards are up to,' said Harry.

Just then their questions were answered, as shells started to fly past their heads. The Boche were at it again.

Harry had been recently appointed Platoon Leader and now had sixteen Diggers under his command, including me.

Harry led George Ruby and Roy Wilson to occupy a large shell hole about fifty yards in front of the Australian line. A shell exploded very close to where they had hunkered down. I was very concerned and decided I should creep over to see if my three cobbers were OK.

I climbed over the parapet and, keeping low, I made my way to the improvised foxhole.

I reached the hole only to find George dismembered with Harry under his good mate's shattered body, shell shocked and covered in George's blood and brain matter. Roy was sitting with his hands holding his head.

I tried to reason with Harry.

'Mate, come on. George's dead; let's get you back to safety. There's a nice meal and a bath waiting for you behind the lines.'

'I'm not leaving George.'

'He'll be all right. We need to get you back.'

'I'm not leaving him behind.'

'Cobber, he's dead. Nothing you or I can do to change that.

'He was my best mate,' said Harry with tears flowing down his face.

'I promise we'll bring him back and we can bury him properly. Just for now it's too dangerous but when the barrage has stopped you and I can come back and get him.'

'You promise?'

'I promise.'

I pushed George off Harry and helped him back to the line. He was taken to a dressing station where they diagnosed him with shell shock. He was taken back to the field hospital. Harry did recover, or so he was told, He was back with his battalion four weeks later. It was obvious to all his cobbers he was still suffering shell shock.

Margaret, You now know how your beloved brother and my great cobber got the way he is now. I will do anything to help him recover.

40

It is my intention to travel to Melbourne on business in April 1921. I would like to visit my old mate and see if I can help in any way.

Can you write to me and let me know if it would be convenient?

Yours sincerely

Peter Bellamy.

Margaret showed the letter to her mother and father, Bernie, while the family was eating dinner.

'Well, I can't see how it would hurt, in fact it may do Harry some good to see his old cobber,' Margaret said.

'What do you think, Harry? Would you like to see your good mate Peter again?' asked Bernie.

Harry didn't stop eating his dinner. He showed no response whatsoever.

'Write back to this Peter, and tell him he's most welcome to make a visit, Margaret,' said Bernie.

'I will.'

COBBERS

CHAPTER 7

April 23

Peter Bellamy caught the train from Sydney to Melbourne. He was sound asleep when the steam train pulled into the Albury train station. He was woken by the guard informing him he had thirty minutes to change over to the Victorian train. The two state governments, in their infinite wisdom, built their tracks using different gauges.

Bellamy was in good company as others more notable than he had also been inconvenienced by changing trains at Albury.

The long list of great Albury train-changers includes Sir Edmund Barton, first Australian Prime Minister, Agatha Christie (1920), the Duke of Cornwall (later King George V, 1901), Arthur Conan Doyle (1920), Prince Henry, Duke of Gloucester (1934), D.H. Lawrence (1922), Rudyard Kipling (1891), Dame Nellie Melba (1931), Robert Louis Stevenson (1890), Mark Twain (1895), H.G. Wells (1939) and the Duke of York (later King George VI, 1927).

Once he settled into the Victorian train, he dozed until reaching Spencer Street Station at 10 am. He had booked into the Windsor Hotel.

Bellamy caught a taxi to the hotel and checked into his suite.

He didn't have much time to rest as he had an appointment with the hypnotherapist at 2 pm.

Doctor Joseph Wright had decided early in his medical career to become a hypnotherapist. He had been a doctor on the Western Front during the war and, apart from the horrendous wounds he treated, the number of shell shock victims astounded him.

He decided to investigate alternative treatments. The most common solution was to send the unfortunate soldiers back into the fray. In their state of mind, many died in battle without firing a shot.

He studied under the renowned psychologist William McDougal, who pioneered hypnosis as a treatment for shell shock. After twelve months in London, he returned to Australia and established a clinic in Melbourne.

The hypnotherapy clinic was located at 287 Collins Street. It was named The Melbourne Hypnotherapy Clinic.

Collins Street Melbourne 1920

Peter arrived five minutes early and the receptionist asked him to take a seat in the waiting room. The room was aptly named. He had to wait forty-five minutes. Finally, he was asked to enter the consulting room.

Sitting behind a large red cedar desk was Dr Wright. He stood up and greeted Peter with a firm handshake.

'Mr Bellamy, I believe you are here to discuss a friend of yours who suffers from shell shock?'

'Yes, that's correct, Dr Wright. We fought in Gallipoli and on the Western Front together.'

'Are you aware when he first suffered the affliction?'

'I am. I was with him, sir.'

'Do you mind telling me what happened?'

Peter described the situation at Mouquet Farm and how Harry's best friend George had been blown to bits.

'I see. I can understand what brought on his condition. What are his symptoms?'

'I haven't seen him yet, but I'm told he doesn't speak. He just stares off into the distance.'

'Do you think he would be willing to see me?'

'I hope so.'

'When will you know?'

'I'm going to visit him after I leave here. I hope seeing me might trigger some memories.'

'Right, well contact my receptionist to make an appointment once you know if he's willing to undergo treatment.'

Bellamy returned to the Windsor and telephoned Margaret from his room.

'Hello, Margaret; it's Peter.'

'Hello, Peter. When do I get to meet you in person?'

'I was hoping tomorrow, seeing it's Saturday.'

'Yes, that would be perfect.'

'Excellent, but how's Harry today?'

'Just the same, I'm afraid.'

'I met a gentleman today who might be able to help. I'll tell you about him tomorrow.'

'That sounds encouraging. I look forward to meeting you and hearing your news.'

Peter ate in the hotel dining room and retired early, looking forward to an uninterrupted sleep.

After breakfast, Peter caught a tram to Bent Street, Northcote. He walked down the tree-lined street until he found Harry's house, number 18. He knocked on the front door and waited.

18 Bent Street Northcote

The front door opened. Standing in front of Peter was one of the most beautiful women he had ever seen. He was taken aback initially and then found his voice.

'Hello, Margaret I'm Peter. I'm very pleased to meet you.'

'Hello, Peter it's a pleasure. Please come inside and meet the family.'

Margaret's mother and father were sitting at the kitchen table. After the introductions, Peter inquired as to Harry's whereabouts.

'We thought it would be best for you to see one other for the first time alone. Margaret will take you out to the front veranda and then get Harry.'

Peter sat in one of the wicker chairs; not Harry's chair, as that would be confrontational.

A few minutes later, Harry appeared on Margaret's arm. He was dressed in his khakis. He sat down with Margaret's help without uttering a word.

'G'day Harry. It's Peter— your old mate from your army days.'

Harry didn't acknowledge his old friend. He just looked ahead with his 1000-yard stare.

'You look great, cobber. You have obviously been keeping fit. Roy and Bill send their regards. They intend to visit you in the near future.

'Crikey mate, we've been through a lot together. We met on the *Ceramic* when we sailed from Albany to Egypt. Do you remember the two up games we used to play? You and I cleaned up. Some of the bastards accused us of cheating. You knocked out one of our accusers' front teeth.

'What about Egypt? Hot stinking place it was although we all enjoyed climbing the pyramids.

'Do you remember the five of us going into Cairo one night? We ended up in a bar and got half pissed. Some bloody Pommy officer walked in and closed the place down for the night. You told him he was a Pommy bastard and hightailed out of there. He ordered two MPs to chase you down but you outran them through the markets. I think you finally got back to camp at about 2 am.'

Harry just kept staring ahead. He showed no reaction at all.

'Then there was Gallipoli. Nobody could forget that shit hole. You, George and Roy, sat next to each other in the landing boat. I was opposite you with Bill.

'I'll never forget the steamboats towing us off towards what would become known as Anzac Cove. The noise from the battlefield was deafening. You looked at me with fear in your eyes.

"Peter, I'm a bit scared, mate," you said.

"We'll be right, mate. Just keep your head low, and listen out for bullets coming your way."

"How the hell will I know bullets are coming my way?"

"Don't worry son, you'll know."

'About four hundred metres from the beach the steamers cut our boats loose, and Roy and the other oarsman began to row. By this time we were close enough for the Turkish machine gun bullets to hit their targets.

'Bill hadn't said anything since entering the boat, which was unusual for him.

"Hey Bill, are you all right, mate?" you asked.

"Yeah, I'm okay; just a little scared."

"We all are, mate. Don't worry about that; bloody hell how could we not be?"

'The boat neared the shore. You looked around at the rest of the diggers in the craft and couldn't believe it. At least ten of the forty who started out on the short journey had been killed, and at least another five or six had severe wounds. You were devastated, Harry, as we all were.

'When Captain Jones gave the order to disembark we ran for the bottom of the cliffs where the first wave had established some sort of a beachhead.

'Harry, you were the first to jump out. You disappeared under the water, which was about five feet deep. The weight of your pack made it very difficult for you to make your way. You finally found a footing and waded towards the stony beach. Once on dry ground, we all ran as best we could with a wet uniform and a pack that weighed over forty pounds dry. God knows how heavy it was wet. All five of us made it to the cliff without being shot. The same could not be said for the rest of the Battalion. Over one hundred men either died in the boats or on the beach, cut down by a ferocious Turkish defence.

'We were instructed to move to the left flank of the beachhead and then to move inland to support our comrades who had landed in the early morning. By the time we began to climb, darkness had descended over the beach, bringing a dark curtain over the dead and wounded.

'Harry you were a hero, mate.'

Harry showed a glimmer of emotion not much but enough to encourage Peter.

He decided that Harry could benefit from visiting Dr Wright even if it was just a slight chance Harry would recover.

Peter discussed it with Harry's family and they all agreed it was worth a try. Peter had insisted that he pay for the treatments.

Peter returned to the Winsor and telephoned Dr Wright's practice. An appointment was made for Tuesday of the following week.

HYPNOTIC TRANCE

CHAPTER 8

April 30 1921

Peter had telephoned the Melbourne Hypnotherapy Clinic and arranged an appointment for Harry to see Dr Wright for April 30 at 11 am.

He had asked Margaret to accompany him and Harry. Peter felt Harry would be more at ease with his sister being with him.

Margaret purchased a dark blue suit from Leviathan Menswear along with a tie and a pair of black brogue shoes. The white shirt was from Pelaco. She laid the outfit on Harry's bed while he took a shower. The family plus Peter were drinking tea in the kitchen, looking forward to seeing Harry in his new outfit.

Finally, Harry walked in. The family just looked at one another. Harry had dressed once again in his khakis and was wearing his slouch hat. Not a word was spoken.

The three of them caught the number 151 tram from Northcote to Collins Street in Melbourne.

They walked up Collins Street until they reached number 287. Harry remained calm, showing no reluctance to follow the other two.

Peter guided them to Dr Wright's rooms, announcing their presence to the receptionist. She instructed them to sit while she informed the doctor of their arrival. Unlike Peter's first visit they were not kept waiting long.

'Good morning, my name is Dr Wright and you are?'

'Margaret Preston. I'm Harry's younger sister.'

'Excellent, and you and I have already met, Mr Bellamy.'

They settled into seats and the doctor began, 'Let me explain my methodology when dealing with shell shock victims. I believe, and in fact, I have proved, that shell shock can be cured through cognitive and effective reintegration. I believe Harry has attempted to manage his traumatic experience at Mouquet Farm by repressing any memory of George's horrific death.

'Harry's symptoms, i.e. silence and staring ahead, are the product of an unconscious process designed to maintain the dissociation. My method relies on Harry reviving his memory of George's death through hypnotherapy. A number of sessions will be required.

'Do you both understand?'

'I think so,' said Margaret.

'What about you, Mr Bellamy?'

'Yes, I think what you are saying is if Harry relives the event enough times he will be able to handle the memory.'

'In essence, that's what I'm saying. I'll have to ask you both to leave while I hypnotise Harry.'

'How long do you think you'll be, Doctor?' asked Margaret.

'That really depends on Harry, I'm afraid.'

Peter and Margaret left the room and sat down once again in the waiting room.

Dr Wright pulled out a glass lens and asked Harry to follow the movement with his eyes. The hypnotist was pleased with the way Harry followed the object.

Dr Wright began to speak in a quiet monotone voice.

'Your eyes are becoming heavy…'

After a few minutes, Dr Wright was satisfied that Harry had entered a hypnotic trance.

He took Harry back to Mouquet Farm so that he could relive the events including George's horrendous death. By the end of the initial session, Harry was speaking and demonstrating great emotion.

Dr Wright ended the session with the clap of his hands.

Peter and Margaret were invited back into the consulting room.

'It went very well. Harry spoke and showed emotion when I guided him into the foxhole.'

'He spoke? My God that's wonderful, a miracle!' said Margaret.

'Don't be too excited. He has reverted to his old self. It will take several sessions before we can claim your brother is healed. However, I should say this has been a very encouraging beginning.'

Peter decided to extend his stay in Melbourne in the hope that Harry could be healed after a few more sessions. He was confident his assistant manager would be able to manage the hotel in Bondi, which he inherited from his parents soon after he returned from the war.

Peter and Harry would attend two sessions a week at the clinic. Peter noticed an improvement after each session. After five weeks, Harry was communicating with his family. Dr Wright declared him cured and ready to re-join society.

Harry had been a teller with the Commonwealth Bank before the war. The bank agreed to take him back. He met his future wife while working in the bank's head office. He married Joy Saunders on June 6 1924 they had two children, a boy and a girl. Harry received several promotions over the years and retired as senior accountant in 1955.

CHAPTER 9

London 1914

Walter Jordan was the youngest of eight children raised in a two-storey terrace house on London's East Side.

The eldest was Henry, 19, and then came Sam, 18, Norman, 17, Emily, 16, and Joan, 15, twins Elizabeth and Margaret, 14, and finally, Walter, 13.

Britain had declared war against the German and Austrian aggressors and everybody in the East End was speculating on what would happen next. Was it going to be a quick and nasty war or would it last until Christmas?

Young Walter worked with his older brothers on the docks. It was hard physical labour but with little education, it was about the best they could do.

Their father, William Jordan, was a police officer. He hoped his sons would follow his vocation one day but at the moment there was very little recruitment going on. Victoria, their mother, was an intelligent woman who encouraged all her children to read and learn about the world, firmly believing this would improve their lot in life despite their lack of formal education.

Saturday, August 15th 1914

The Jordan family were sitting around the dining room table. Traditionally, the family ate their roast dinner on a Saturday night.

After the dishes were cleared, washed, and dried by the children, they were free to go off to the local dance or pool hall, depending on their preference.

This particular Saturday night the patriarch of the family made an announcement.

'As you are all aware, there's a war going on and the Government has asked all able-bodied men to volunteer. After discussing the situation with your mother, I have decided that it is my duty to enlist. It is my intention to attend the army recruitment centre on Monday morning.'

'Good on you, Father, I think it's very noble of you,' said Emily.

'Thank you, Emily.'

'I was thinking seriously of enlisting too, and now that you are going I've made my mind up,' said Henry.

'Me too,' said Sam.

'Well, Norman and Walter, you'll be the men of the household. I expect you to take care of your mother and sisters while we are away. Mind you, I don't think it will be for that long.'

Unknown to his parents, Norman had already enlisted, lying about his age. He was due to report to Wellington Barracks on Monday morning. He decided to keep quiet now and write his parents a letter to be read after he'd left the house.

Victoria was supportive of William going off to war, but far less enthusiastic about seeing two of her sons follow him. She resolved herself to the fact and would pray daily they all returned without injury.

Walter went out into the small back yard behind the tool shed and lit up a cigarette he had pinched from his father's pack. It didn't seem fair that his older brothers were heading off to the ultimate adventure while he and Norman stayed at home with the girls.

Monday, August 17th 1914

Victoria was in the kitchen making sure all her children were making their breakfast. The girls worked together in the sugar refinery and were due to start at 7.30am. Norm hadn't yet shown his face so Emily was sent to the boys' room to get him moving. Emily returned downstairs clutching Norm's short note that explained he had joined the army and would write soon.

This was too much for Victoria. After the other children set off for work, she sat down and sobbed, consumed by fear about her husband and three boys fighting in a horrible war. What if one of them was killed, or, God forbid, all of them?

William was angry that Norm hadn't consulted him about enlisting. However, he understood his son's motivation to fight for King and country.

He gathered Henry and Sam and they made their way to the recruitment office. As they approached the building, they saw a line of men waiting outside the door.

'Looks like we're in for a long wait, lads. This war is more popular than I thought.'

After queuing for two hours, the Jordan men entered the recruitment office, a hive of activity with blokes being examined by doctors and others being measured for uniforms. A tall burly sergeant approached William and asked his age. Without hesitation William lied, saying he was forty-two, when actually, he was forty-nine.

All three were processed and accepted. Delighted, they headed to the *Black Swan* for celebratory ale.

'Well Pa, we're up to our necks now. I hope we made the right decision,' said Henry, sipping his pint.

'It's too late to start doubting now son, maybe you should have decided to stay home with your sisters.'

'Don't get me wrong, Pa, I thought long and hard before I decided to enlist. It's just a little daunting, that's all.'

'I know how Henry feels, Pa. It's not that we regret signing up, it's just the thought of killing another human being, Krauts or otherwise.'

'Yeah and trying to avoid German bullets and shells,' said Henry.

'I understand, boys. War is no picnic and I'm sure we'll all see and experience terrible things. Now we've enlisted we have to be positive and if you have any misgivings, don't let them be known to anyone; keep them to yourselves. Being a police officer all these years has taught me never to divulge your true feelings to anybody. Others will see this as a weakness.'

The next two weeks were spent getting their affairs in order. As a police sergeant, William was released by the force with the assurance he could have his old position back when the war was over.

Although the two boys worked consistently at the docks, they were casual labour, so there were no guarantees about future jobs. Henry and Sam weren't too worried as they hoped for better career options when they returned.

August 21st 1914

The Jordan family gathered around the long table for their last meal as a family for some time.

'Well everybody, as you know Henry, Sam and I are leaving tomorrow morning to begin our training. I don't know when we'll all be at the same table again but I'm hopeful of Christmas dinner together. Young Norm has headed off before us. He'll probably greet us when we get to France. Walter, as the man of the house, you must look after your sisters and mother.'

'I think it will more like us looking after Walter and trying to keep him out of mischief,' said Emily.

All the other girls giggled, agreeing with Emily.

'Don't you listen to them, Walter. I have total faith in you.'

'Thanks, Pa.'

'Your mother has cooked a magnificent bird so let's all enjoy the meal. I've got a strong feeling it will be our last tasty dinner for quite a while; the army isn't known for its food.'

'Don't be getting yourself shot over there, Father, we simply couldn't bear it,' said Elizabeth.

'That's right, Father, keep your head down. We need you back here when this horrid war is over,' agreed Margaret.

'Don't worry, girls. I've survived as a policeman all these years. A few Germans aren't going to give me any trouble. We'll be fine, won't we lads?'

Henry nodded. 'Of course we will Pa, we know how to take care of ourselves.'

The next day, after a tearful farewell, the trio of Jordan men departed for Chelsea Barracks to undergo eight weeks of basic training.

The normal day's regime began with Reveille at 5.30am. This didn't worry William and the boys; they were used to getting up at this hour. The first task of the day was to tidy up and clean the hut, and once finished, they could enjoy a cup of tea.

Next, the focus was on improving fitness among the new recruits with marching on the parade ground for an hour and a half. They then had breakfast. The remainder of the morning was spent drilling on the parade ground, learning to march correctly, form fours and about turn. Between 12.15pm and 2pm, the men took lunch before returning for more drills until 4.15pm. The unlucky few might be detailed off for fatigues or work parties thereafter but otherwise, recruits were off-duty although often required to spend time cleaning kit and shining boots.

'Dad, when do you think we'll be trained on the correct way to fire our rifles and other such things that might keep us alive when we get to the front?'

'Don't worry, son, I reckon we've done enough marching. The time for some real training is very near.'

'I bloody hope so; this isn't what I signed up for. And another thing, when do you reckon we'll get our uniforms? I'm sick of wearing the same bloody clothes every day.'

'You've just got to be a little patient, Henry, it will happen.'

Sure enough, training soon switched to correct ways to move in the field, including night operations.

Weapon handling skills covered the use of bayonet and hand grenades. Hours were spent practising marksmanship and the correct method to dig a trench; this training would prove very useful when they were at the front.

From 2.30pm on the weekends, the recruits played various recreational games including soccer and rugby.

The two Jordan boys were sitting in the mess hut, having just finished their dinner.

'So, mate, what do you think of army life so far?'

'Well, now that we're shooting rifles and such, not too bad.'

'Do you miss Jane?'

'What a stupid fucking question, Sam. Of course, I miss her, I love her.'

'Sorry mate… you're right, it was a stupid question. Do you reckon you'll marry her when you get back?'

'Yeah, I've got to get back first. Have you read the latest casualty figures? Bloody frightening. And what about you? Last I heard you were taking out a beautiful redhead.'

'I don't know, I've got a feeling she won't be around by the time we get back.'

'Why not, mate?'

'Her name is Anna. You're right— she is beautiful, and beautiful girls get taken if you leave them alone. She did say she'd wait for me so, you never know your luck.'

October 16th 1914

At last, the day came when William, Henry and Sam Jordan joined the rest of the recruits for the Passing Out Ceremony and graduation from basic training. The Jordans all became soldiers in the London Regiment 5th London Brigade.

Because William had been a sergeant in the Police Force the Commander of the barracks promoted him to sergeant.

William endeavoured to find out which regiment his son Norm had been posted to but so far his enquiries had been unsuccessful.

Five days leave was granted before they shipped to France. William and his two sons arrived at the family home resplendent in their khaki uniforms.

Their days were spent with family, friends, and sweethearts.

Sam, William, and Henry Jordan

Henry and Sam made the most of their time with their respective girlfriends.

Henry organised a romantic dinner at a little café in East London. They both chose fish and chips with a side salad. Beer was their drink of choice.

'Jane, when I return from the war would you consider marrying me?'

'Henry, I would be honoured to be your wife.'

'Right, wonderful, excellent that's settled then.'

'There's only one thing, darling.'

'Oh, and what's that?'

'You've got to come home alive.'

'I'll certainly do my best, sweetheart.'

Holding hands, they left dinner, heads swimming with thoughts of their future lives together.

Sam took Anna to the cinema where the main feature was *The Italian*, directed by Reginald Barker.

Anna didn't think much of the film but Sam quite enjoyed it.

They had a coffee on the way home.

'Anna, do you think we have a future together?'

'Well, Sam it's hard to say, what with you going off to war and all.'

'Assuming I come back in one piece, would you marry me then?'

'Sam darling, just come back and then we can talk about it.'

Sam walked her home and kissed her farewell. He was not at all confident that he would ever see her again; Anna could well be married by the time he returned, if he ever did.

William and Victoria lay in bed holding hands, both aware they would not make love again for a very long time.

'William, promise me you will come home safely. And make sure Henry and Sam are with you.'

'Darling, I will come home unscathed and will take care of our boys. Chances are, by the time we get over there, the war will be over.'

'I certainly hope so. Should I make you wait until your return to make love again?'

'I have no control over how long this war will go on for, my darling.'

'That's true, come here.'

The next morning the two brothers said goodbye to their mother, sisters and little brother. William hugged his wife, reiterating his promise to return as they departed to join their battalion at barracks.

October 18th 1914

The 5th London Regiment marched to the dock at Southampton and boarded several troop ships bound for Marseilles.

Conditions were hot and cramped and with many of the men suffering from seasickness, it was often a fight to reach the hand railing.

After what seemed an eternity, the ships pulled into Marseilles, where the majority of the soldiers could not wait to feel the earth under their feet.

Their journey continued by train up to Belgium and a city called Ypres. Most of the troops had never heard of Ypres, let alone know how to pronounce it correctly.

Again, conditions were cramped on the train, but at least they didn't have rough seas to contend with.

So far, the Jordan men had been able to stick together and it was reassuring for Henry and Sam to have their father by their side.

Two days before the 5th London Regiment arrived, fighting began. This became known as the First Battle of Ypres.

Ypres October 29th 1914
The Cloth Hall and Cathedral

Troops were assembled at the railway siding ready to march into Ypres. There seemed no visible fighting although they could hear artillery in the distance.

1st London Brigade Marching into Ypres

THE PRODIGAL SON

CHAPTER 10

Norm Jordan arrived in Marseilles on October 2nd 1914, two weeks before his father and brothers. He hadn't enjoyed the short sea journey at all, as the ship was cramped and he became seasick immediately the swells began.

He, along with his battalion, The Royal Fusiliers, were then loaded on trains to join their countrymen at Ypres in the Flanders region of Belgium.

Norm, a shy boy who typically found it difficult to make friends, had met and befriended a fellow called James Hargreaves. Despite completely different backgrounds, they got on extremely well. James' middle-class family included a father who was a doctor and a mother who was a nurse. James had also lied about his age to enlist, sharing the same birthday as Norm.

They arrived at Ypres on October 14, at last able to stretch their legs and walk around the pretty town dominated by the Cloth House and the Cathedral beside it.

Sightseeing was soon replaced by the horror of combat - the two boys were about to partake in the 1st Battle of Ypres.

1st Battle of Ypres

On October 19th near the north Belgian city of Ypres, Allied and German forces began the first of three battles to control the city and its advantageous coastal position during this First World War.

After the Germans advanced through Belgium and eastern France with minimal resistance, their great push was curtailed in late September, 1914, by a decisive Allied victory in the Battle of Marne. The 'Race to the Sea' began as each army attempted to outflank the other on their way northwards, hastily constructing trench fortifications as they went. The race ended in mid-October at Ypres, the ancient Flemish city with its fortifications guarding the ports of the English Channel and beyond, the North Sea.

Following the Germans' capture of Antwerp in early October, Belgian forces and troops of the British Expeditionary Force commanded by Sir John French withdrew to Ypres, arriving at the city between October 8th and 19th to reinforce the Belgian and French defences. Meanwhile, the Germans prepared to launch the first phase of an offensive aimed at breaking the Allied lines and capturing Ypres and other channel ports, thus controlling access to the North Sea.

On October 19th, a protracted period of fierce combat began as the Germans opened their Flanders offensive. The Allies steadfastly resisted while seeking their own chances to go on the attack wherever possible. Fighting continued with heavy losses on both sides.

The Allied forces suffered 7,960 deaths, 29,563 wounded and 17,875 missing, presumed dead. Winter weather forced the battle and killing to a halt. The area on the British side to Menin, and Roulers on the German side became known as the Ypres Salient, a region that would see some of the war's bitterest and most brutal struggles over the next few years.

Norm and his mate James were billeted out in a farmhouse on the outskirts of Ypres. The Belgium family who cared for them were very nice although neither boy could speak Flemish or French, the two languages spoken in the house.

On the morning of October 19th they woke to the sounds of loud banging on the front door. Mrs Joossens came quickly down the stairs and opened the door. Standing in front of her was a sergeant from the British army.

'Sorry if I woke you, ma'am but I need to collect the two soldiers you have been billeting. Immediately.'

The two boys heard the conversation and came to the door.

'OK, lads, time to go. We've got a war to fight and by all accounts, your war starts today.'

Acknowledging the sergeant, they gathered their packs and said farewell to Mrs Joossens.

The two young soldiers followed their sergeant as he rounded up another twenty or so Royal Fusiliers. It seemed they were all about the same age as Norm and James. They marched through Ypres and headed for the line at Langemarck, a town north of Ypres and neighbouring Passchendaele.

October 21st 1914

At five in the afternoon, the Fusiliers arrived at the front line, facing the German army. The British Commanders were expecting a push from the German 4th Army, and their task was to stop it.

Norm and James sat waiting in the trench, smoking. They'd both recently started, as every other soldier seemed to be a smoker. Whether it alleviated boredom or calmed their nerves, cigarettes were given to them as part of their rations. They were smoking and silent, both very nervous if not terrified.

Unknown to them, in the opposite German trenches were young soldiers not much older than they were. Nicknamed the 'Kinder Korps', these German university students had been willingly seconded into the army to boost the strength of their country's battalions. The German commanders didn't intersperse these young men among older, more experienced soldiers; they banded them together in the one battalion.

Enemy artillery began to rain down on the British positions. At first, their range was inaccurate so they didn't cause too much havoc. However, it didn't take long before the Germans worked out the coordinates and shells were dropping in or close to the Allied trenches. Norm and James witnessed their first casualty – a soldier, only ten yards away, received shrapnel to his neck, almost severing his head. Both boys were in shock but knew they had to pull themselves together.

Captain McDonald, their commander, moved down the trenches alerting troops to the fact that when the barrage ended a charging German army would confront them.

As expected, the barrage ceased. They waited in silence, an acrid smell from shells permeating throughout the trenches. Looking out with a periscope, Captain McDonald saw a mist drifting over no man's land. It was not a mist as he had experienced in his home country of Scotland, but nevertheless a mist. Smoke from the barrage was making it problematic to see more than fifty yards ahead. He saw movement and faintly made out a row of enemy troops making their way to attack the British line. He quickly blew the whistle to alert his troops to the impending attack.

Norm and James looked at each other and nodded as if to say, *we'll be all right, we know how to fight.*

This composed German approach did nothing to calm the butterflies in their stomachs.

The Krauts started to fire their rifles, and machine guns were attacking the trenches. In return, the Allies began to fire back with rifle, machine gun and mortar. The Germans were dropping like flies but more and more kept coming; it was a bloodbath.

A German soldier managed to reach James and Norm's section of the trench and leaped forward to jump in. Norm held up his bayonet and impaled the eighteen-year-old student soldier from Heidelberg. Withdrawing the blade, Norm then shot the wounded soldier to eliminate the obvious pain he was suffering.

Turning to face the onslaught again, Norm glanced towards James only to find his mate slumped over the wall of the trench. He had been hit in the forehead and would've died instantly. This sight made Norm even more determined. The Germans were beginning to retreat and orders were to go after the bastards. Norm climbed the ladder and began to run, firing his 303 at the retreating enemy. He was confident he had killed a few when a German machine gun ripped him apart.

He was the first casualty in the Jordan family, and his mother received a telegram two weeks later. Norm was just seventeen. His father William was not notified for several more weeks.

Norm Jordan

PRIVATE INVESTIGATIONS

CHAPTER 11

Sergeant William Jordan was sitting in a dugout alone. He had a piece of paper in his hand and kept reading the words over and over but couldn't bring himself to believe them.

It is with great regret that we inform you, your son Private Norman Jordan was killed in action near Ypres on 21 October 1914.

What sort of world was it that a son dies before his father? The lad was only seventeen for God sakes.

He would have to try and track down Henry and Sam who had been transferred to the 8th division. He had no idea where they were now located, but he was sure he would find them eventually.

A messenger entered the dugout, interrupting William's sorrowful contemplation. The young soldier handed him an envelope. The note ordered William to report to divisional headquarters in a chateau thirty miles behind the lines in Boulogne, where General John French was based.

Instructed to leave for Boulogne immediately, there would be little time for mourning. A vehicle was already waiting to take him. William grabbed his pack and left.

He arrived at the port city in the afternoon and was shown his quarters, an army tent large enough to accommodate four officers, but in this instance, for him alone.

He ate his evening meal in the mess tent and retired at 9pm.

Reveille was at five thirty, breakfast at eight. William waited around for someone to inform him why he had been summoned; finally, at 10am a captain introduced himself and asked William to accompany him to the quarters of Lieutenant Colonel Francis Oats.

'Sergeant William Jordan, sir,' Captain Harris said.

'Oh good, come on in sergeant, would you care for a cup of tea?'

'Yes, sir, that would be very nice.'

'While my orderly organises things let me pass on my sympathy for the loss of your young son. Terrible thing.'

'Thank you, sir. Yes, it is very difficult to accept losing a son so young.'

'Yes, no doubt it is. Now Jordan, I believe you were a sergeant in the London Police, homicide squad I believe.'

'Yes sir, I had twenty years with the force and God willing I'll return to policing when the war is over.'

'Sterling. I am sure they will be happy to have you back. Sergeant, the reason I'm interested in your police background is we've had a terrible murder in Poperinge, a Captain Pittard. He was responsible for the logistics of all goods coming and going at the warehouses. You can appreciate this is a critical role.'

'Are you asking me for some advice on how to go about capturing the perpetrators, sir?'

'Well no, I'm asking for a little more than that. I want you to be Captain Pittard's replacement. The plan is getting you inside to find the information we need to bring these murderous bastards to justice.'

'You say these as if there is more than one of them. May I ask what brings you to that conclusion?'

'My suspicion is that a major smuggling ring is involved. Captain Pittard may well have discovered who they were and what they were up to. I believe that's why he was murdered. Your orders are to report to the Poperinge warehouse as the new officer in charge. I will promote you to Captain, a rank you will retain for the war's duration. There is one catch. We need to make sure nobody knows your background so you will be deleted from all war records and army records. From now on you are Captain William Sykes of the 60th London Division. This of, course, means you will be listed as "missing". Your wife will be informed as such, as will your two sons fighting over here.'

'Is that absolutely necessary, sir? My wife and family will be devastated.'

'I'm afraid it is, captain; there can be no argument. The success of the mission depends on it.'

'Yes sir, when should I leave for Poperinge, sir?

'Tomorrow, and you need to be fitted out with a new uniform and such.'

'I take it I report directly to you, sir?'

'That's correct, captain, I expect weekly reports.'

'Thank you, sir.'

'Go and find these bastards, captain, we're all relying on you.'

William saluted and departed for his tent. He had a lot to think about.

Next morning, his new uniform was delivered. He had to admit to himself that he looked rather smart in a captain's uniform with the three stars on his epaulets.

A staff car collected him for the long journey to Poperinge, a place he had only visited once before. He wasn't very impressed with the troops' drunken behaviour, or their propensity to visit the town's famous brothels. However, William did enjoy visiting Talbot House, a place where he could relax and chat with other soldiers about their experiences thus far.

Located in the West Flanders region of Belgium, near to the border with France, Poperinge was just behind Allied lines and served as an R&R town for Allied troops. Allied soldiers knew the town as "Pops". Most of the British soldiers who fought on the Western Front passed through Poperinge. The town served as a major British supply base and garrison for the front.

Poperinge also became the hub for informal social life for Allied soldiers, particularly British troops, during the war. "Pops" provided soldiers with a brief reprieve from the harsh life of the trenches and the front. A thriving black market trade developed, with British military supplies being sold at inflated prices. The town also had numerous cafés, estaminets (bars or pubs) and brothels, which were frequented by the troops. Poperinge was a safe place for British troops and supply depots because it lay beyond the range of German artillery.

One of the centres of social life for soldiers in Poperinge during the First World War was Talbot House. Talbot House was established in 1915 as a club for British soldiers by Reverend Philip 'Tubby' Clayton and Chaplain Neville Talbot. Talbot House was named for Chaplain Talbot's younger brother, Lieutenant Gilbert Talbot, who had recently been killed in the vicinity of the nearby villages of Hooge and Zillebeke.

Talbot House

Reverend 'Tubby' Clayton was a short thirty-year-old vicar in the Anglican Church. He had arrived in Belgium in November 1915 and was assigned to serve as the military chaplain to the British 16th Infantry Brigade. The previous chaplain for the 16th Brigade had been killed the month before.

When Reverend Clayton visited Poperinge, he observed that aside from cafés, drinking spots, and houses of prostitution, soldiers had no places to go in the town. Clayton wanted to establish a place for soldiers to gather that was removed from the debauchery that characterised many of the other places that British soldiers frequented.

Arriving at Pops, William was driven to a quaint cottage. This was to be his home for the duration of the investigation.

William entered and found a very nice sitting room with a wood-fired slow combustion fire. There was a Chesterfield lounge suite in a rich burgundy colour and a gramophone, together with a sizeable record collection.

'This certainly beats the heck out of the dugout I once called home,' he said aloud.

Upstairs were two bedrooms, tastefully decorated, and a bathroom. He looked out the bedroom window and could see a very well maintained garden with a lawn that had obviously just been mown.

This may well be a very long investigation, he thought.

Poperinge Cottage

After the best night's sleep he had enjoyed since joining up, he sat down to a breakfast of fresh fruit and bread spread with lashings of honey.

Things can only get worse, he thought. I'm sure I will solve this case soon and then I'll be back in the mud. Although… I will be a captain, so I will get a few more privileges.

A knock on the door brought him out of his daydreaming.

'Enter.'

'Sir, I am Sergeant Abbott. I've been instructed to take you to the warehouse complex where your office is located. I am also to show you around the facility and answer any questions you may have, sir.'

'At ease, sergeant. Have you been in this role for long?'

'Since our boys arrived here, sir; that would be September 1914.'

'You reported to Captain Pittard?'

'I did, sir, we arrived here on the same day.'

'What was he like, sergeant?'

'He was a wonderful man, sir, you couldn't find a finer gentleman.'

'Did he have any enemies that you knew of?'

'No sir, he was very popular with all the men. Mind you, if you stepped out of line he'd soon bring you back.'

'So, why on earth would someone want him dead?'

'It's a complete mystery, sir, I really don't know.'

'All right, sergeant, show me where I'll be stationed.'

'Yes sir, follow me, sir.'

The two men left the cottage and stepped into a staff car. The driver was a young private; he didn't look much older than Norm.

They arrived at the warehouse ten minutes later, Sergeant Abbott opened the door for his superior, and they entered what would be William's office.

'This looks perfectly adequate. Have you left Captain Pittard's things untouched?'

'Yes, sir, I can arrange for them to be taken out if you wish.'

'No, don't bother. I may find some things that will help me get started more quickly. You know, procedures he used and so forth.'

'Yes sir, whatever you think is best. Would you care to inspect the warehouses and the below ground munitions store?'

'Yes I would, thank you, sergeant. Lead the way.'

The two men walked into the first storehouse. It was a hive of activity; medical supplies were being packed into wooden boxes ready to be transported to the front. Other supplies, such as tinned food and biscuits, tea and coffee, were also packed into the boxes for shipment.

They walked into the second storehouse and it was a similar scene, with people everywhere packing rifles and uniforms as well as many other sundry items.

The newly created Captain Sykes asked if he could inspect the rail platform where most of the goods arrived for storage and distribution.

Two trains a day arrived at the landing, making the station an assiduous depot.

Not only were the trains hauling cargo they were also used to transport troops.

Unloading Rail Cars

Finally, Captain Sykes inspected the underground weapon storage, the most important facility to support the war effort.

'Have there been any accidents while handling the shells etc., sergeant?'

'I'm afraid so sir, we lose about one or two of our finest every month.'

'Surely we can improve procedures to minimise accidents happening.'

'Captain Pittard tried implementing all sorts of safety measures but to no avail.'

'Well, I'm certainly going to try my hardest to reduce these accidents.'

'Yes, sir.'

When you think of the numbers we're losing each day on the front, a couple each month pales into insignificance, thought Sergeant Abbott.

'Right then. I think I'll walk back to my office and try and get my head around the operation. I won't need you for the remainder of the day sergeant. By the way, what do you actually do?'

'I check the manifests against the goods received in store one, sir.'

'Are there ever any anomalies? You know, goods listed but not supplied?'

'Not generally, sir. There is a very small amount of pilfering but generally, all the goods are present and accounted for.'

William entered his office and sat down at the oak desk; the chair was one that swivelled, and he'd never sat in a chair quite like it. On the desk was a silver frame with a photo of a very attractive woman, Captain

Pittard's wife or sweetheart, he thought. He placed it carefully in the desk's bottom drawer. He looked around the office. Everything had its place and was very neat. His predecessor was obviously a very fastidious man, he thought.

He got up and opened the top drawer of the filing cabinet; files were in alphabetical order, making it easier to find a particular file. William decided that he needed to go through each file carefully to determine if they contained any clues to Pittard's demise.

He grabbed a bunch, A to G, and sat back down at his desk. Most of them were routine manifests for shipments, personnel records and various other sundry matters. By the end of the day, he had read every file up to T. His eyes were watering and he found it difficult to focus. Time to call it a day, he thought. He rang the driver who came immediately and drove him home to the cottage.

When he entered the sitting room he noticed a decanter. He sniffed its contents, and, sure enough, it was scotch. Bloody hell, the life of a captain is a charmed one, he thought.

After pouring himself a glass, he sat in the leather wingback and contemplated the day.

Nothing seemed suspicious; nor did any particular person stand out. His thoughts of a long investigation may well prove to be true.

There had to be a reason why one or more parties decided they had to murder Pittard. He had probably discovered a racket or something. Time would tell, and he was determined to solve this murder. His nickname in the force was Bulldog.

BULLDOG

CHAPTER 12

Weeks passed with William sending regular reports to Lieutenant Colonel Oats as required, but really there was little to tell. He reported that Captain Pittard was a well-respected officer who appeared to have no enemies. Spot-checking the manifests against the cargo hadn't exposed any pilfering. He also investigated whether Captain Pittard had a mistress but by all accounts, he remained faithful to his wife back home. Despite the hunch that Pittard had uncovered a racket, to date no such racket had been uncovered.

May 1915

Henry and Sam had survived their first combat mission, The Second Battle of Ypres.

The battle began in April 1915, a German plan developed to divert Allied attention away from the Eastern Front. It was also the first battle where the Germans used chlorine gas. The Allies drove the Germans back to their lines, a failure for the Germans and victory for the Allies. As a result of this unsuccessful attack, the German army gave up its attempts to take the town, choosing instead to demolish it by means of constant bombardment. By the end of the war, Ypres had been largely destroyed.

Ypres 1917

The two Jordan boys were given leave and chose to spend it in Poperinge. They had witnessed horrible carnage and injury, including the effects of the German gas. Both felt fortunate to have survived and were now intent on enjoying themselves for a while.

The brothers were walking through the busy town centre when they noticed an officer's limousine. To their amazement, their father William was riding in the back. This was confusing, for the boys were still coming to grips with the fact their father was listed as missing, presumed dead.

Sam jumped up and down and waved to his father, as did Henry. The officer glanced in their direction and then continued to read the document he was holding.

'What the fuck! That was Pa, I'm sure of it,' yelled Sam.

'I know, mate, that was him, for fuck's sake I know my own father. What in God's name is going on?'

'Let's go to headquarters and see if we can get to the bottom of this,' said Henry.

The bewildered young soldiers visited HQ and explained their experience to the officer on duty. Obligingly he checked the records but couldn't even find Sergeant Jordan listed as missing. As far as he could tell there had never been such a person registered in the British Army.

The Jordan boys left the offices dejected and even further confused. Rather than visit a brothel, they decided to get some advice from Tubby over at Talbot House.

Meanwhile, William was sitting in his office trying not to weep. The sight of his two sons waving excitably had a devastating effect on him. He was seriously considering calling Lieutenant Colonel Oats and pleading to be taken off the case. He looked down at his desk, and noticed a handwritten note, folded over twice. All his mail arrived in envelopes so this was highly unusual.

He opened it up and began to read.

Dear Captain Sykes,

I can't divulge my identity for fear of retribution, but I know what happened to Captain Pittard, or, I should say, I know why they killed him.

Captain Pittard uncovered a crime ring operating in the Poperinge storehouses.

I know you have been monitoring the manifests and checking that all goods listed are accounted for. This has given you a false interpretation.

What has actually been happening is that the manifests are altered en route. Sailors in the merchant fleet are paid significant amounts to forge manifests.

The goods I specifically refer to are medical supplies, mainly morphine. Once the ships are unloaded the 'extra' morphine is stolen, leaving only the amount listed on the falsified manifest.

The morphine is then loaded into ballast crates and shipped back to where it came from originally; America. Gangs from New York then sell it either as morphine or heroin, a more refined form of the drug. Apparently, there are huge sums of money to be made on the black market.

Captain Pittard became suspicious and organised for a military policeman to go undercover as a merchant seaman. It was while this policeman was on board that he discovered the scam.

The gang in Poperinge involves all levels. A fellow officer, one of the gang, informed the leaders that Captain Pittard was about to arrest the gang leaders. They got in first and eliminated him.

I am putting my own life in danger by divulging the gang leaders but I owe it to Captain Pittard and the boys at the front that aren't getting the morphine they need.

The three major leaders are:

Sergeant Abbott
Major Thomas Albright
Corporal Bernard Bennett

Sir, I wish you every success in your endeavours.

Anonymous

William reread the letter; astonished that Sergeant Abbott, his right-hand man, was one of the gang leaders. He had to be very careful about how the situation was handled. Abbott had been privy to information and could prove to be dangerous. William had not divulged his true reason for replacing Pittard, but nevertheless...

This letter changed his mind about requesting to be excused from the case. If in fact, the accusations were correct, the case would soon be solved and William could return to his family and divulge the truth about his recent role.

He had to decide whether this week's report to Oats mentioned what he had just learned before actually verifying it as truth. No, it was better not to, as a proved case was far preferable to speculation based on an anonymous letter.

WHERE'S MY DAD?

CHAPTER 13

April 1916 - London

Walter Jordan continued working on the docks while the war raged on and everyone else seemed to be fighting for King and country. When he learned his brother Norm had been killed, he and the rest of the family were devastated.

Two long years had passed since Walter had seen his father and brothers. What if he never saw them again? He loved his mother and sisters, but being the only male in the household was difficult at times.

Walter had been contemplating sneaking away to enlist in the army; surely a better chance of catching up with everyone if he was over there too.

A final decision was made on a Monday morning in April. Before the rest of the family woke, Walter slipped out the front door and headed for the army recruitment office. He had a little time to kill before the doors opened, so he walked down to the Thames and along the bank, taking a seat on a bench overlooking the river. The city of London was on the other side. Walter asked himself some appropriate questions such as, 'Do you really want to do this?' The answers were all affirmative. Looking at his watch he realised it was time to return to the recruitment centre.

There were only a few other men waiting, a sharp contrast to 1914 and the two-hour queues for enlisting.

The doors opened punctually, and a tall skinny sergeant greeted the potential recruits.

'Good morning gentlemen. Make your way inside and we'll get you all processed.'

When it was time for Walter to declare his age he responded confidently.

'Eighteen, sir.'

The recruitment officer looked Walter up and down.

'Right, well, you'll do. Sign these documents and go into the next room to be sized up for your uniform.'

Walter did as he was instructed, the first of many orders he would have to obey throughout his army career.

He felt a pang of guilt about not leaving a letter for his mother, but, he knew she would contact the authorities and reveal his true age. Even with the catastrophic casualties the Allies were enduring in France and Belgium, they wouldn't take a fifteen-year-old boy.

It would be easier to write from the front once he had settled in.

The next stage in Walter's military career was training camp at Chelsea Barracks, the same place his dad and brothers had attended.

Normally, new recruits trained for eight weeks but with the need for reinforcements, this was reduced to six weeks, barely enough time to learn correct marching, let alone how to fire a rifle accurately.

June 1st 1916

Walter boarded the troop ship *Esperance* that would take him and his pals to war. They berthed at Marseilles and were immediately taken to the railway platform for the train journey to Poperinge.

The town was abuzz with soldiers; trucks and horses coming and going through the cobblestone streets.

His battalion, the 19th London Brigade, were accommodated in a tent city behind the village itself. During their two days in Pops, some of the older soldiers frequented the famous brothels but Walter found Talbot House more to his liking. There was a visitor's book, which he meticulously scanned to see if his father and brothers had been there. Sure enough, he found entries by all three and reading their entries really lifted his spirits.

December 1914

What a wonderful haven to get away from the war and just relax and contemplate.

Thank you, Tubby.

Sergeant William Jordan

December 1914

Thank you Tubby, enjoyed the tea and the long chat we had.
Private Henry Jordan

December 1914

I really enjoyed this place Tubby. Thank you.
Private Sam Jordan

Walter was delighted the three other Jordans were still together. They really had been able to look out for each other.

The brigade assembled in the main square of Poperinge to be loaded on London buses and taken to the Somme valley in preparation for a major push against the Bosch.

Everybody felt a real sense of excitement. At last, they would have the opportunity to blast the hell out of the Germans.

The trip to the Somme took four days through mud, ice, and snow. It wasn't particularly comfortable but beat the heck out of marching with a sixty-pound pack on your back.

Walter wondered whether his father and brothers would be taking part in this same battle. He was awestruck by everything around him. Huge guns lined the entire front facing the German lines, men were carrying ammunition boxes into the support trenches, and horses were hauling

Howitzers into position. Soldiers were everywhere he looked. Walter had no idea how many. In actual fact, thirteen divisions, around 150,000 men, took part in the first day of the Battle of the Somme.

Front Line Artillery at the Somme

Walter's battalion was ordered to report to Major Thomas at operational headquarters. Major Thomas addressed them, emphasising that the German army would be close to annihilation after the Allied barrage that had taken place for several days now.

'Men, when you go over the top tomorrow morning, our orders from General Haig are to walk purposefully. We do not run. The chance of encountering strong defence is unlikely. You may encounter sporadic fire but it's likely to be minimal. Your commanders will lead you to your positions in the enemies' trench. I wish you Godspeed and may you live to fight another day.'

Moving in formation, the men from the London area marched about a mile to their section of the trench opposite the objective, Gommecourt.

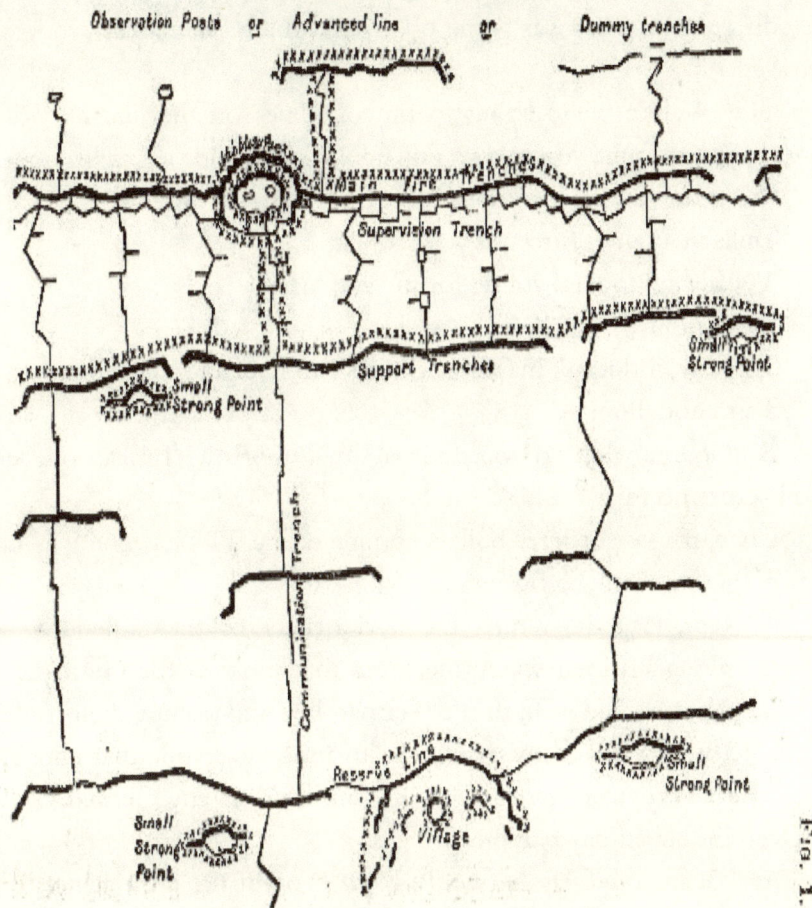

German Defence Line: The Somme

Typically, trench systems consisted of three main fire or support trenches, connected by communication trenches, various posts, strong points, and saps used to tunnel underneath the enemy lines and detonate explosives.

By 1916, the German system of defence had three or four such trench systems layered back over a distance of a couple of miles.

By 1917, the system had deepened even further.

The assaults of 1916 faced defensive systems several miles deep.

June 30ᵗʰ 1916

Noise from the big guns made sleep virtually impossible. Everyone tried to be indifferent to what was going on around them but actually, they were all petrified.

'Hey Walter, we're about to put our lives on the line for King and country. Isn't it time you told us just how fucking old you really are?'

'What do you mean? I'm eighteen just like you, George.'

'Bullshit Walter, fifteen if you're lucky.'

'I've always looked young for my age mate.'

'Yeah right.'

'Anyway, it doesn't matter anymore. I'm here and that's that.'

'Fair enough mate.'

'So George what do you think about tomorrow? I mean our leisurely stroll across no man's land?'

'Mate, if I've got Jerry bullets coming at me, I'll be running as fast as I can. Forget this walking business.'

At 4am, Captain White, the lead officer of the impending attack, moved among his men reassuring them that most of the Germans would be dead. They should walk to the German line and occupy their trenches in the name of Britain and the King. He informed everyone that initially, they would hear seventeen mines explode, finishing off any Germans who had survived the seven-day barrage.

At 7.30am precisely he would blow his whistle, their signal to climb the ladders and go over the top.

'Sounds like a plan,' said Joe Turner.

'I hope he's bloody right,' muttered George

They would soon find out. The time was 7am.

July 1ˢᵗ 1916

Crouching down in the trench, Walter inspected his Enfield 303 and made sure the bayonet was fastened firmly. He couldn't quite imagine stabbing another human being with a bayonet, but would soon know if he could do it.

Time was ticking over very slowly. It seemed ages since the big guns stopped firing their deadly shells but in fact, only five minutes had passed.

At 7.05am the first of the explosions was heard and felt and then in quick succession another sixteen. The noise and booms knocked soldiers off their feet.

Their time to go over had arrived. Captain White blew his whistle and the first men climbed the ladders and began their walk across no man's land.

German machine guns cut them down.

'I thought the fucking Krauts were all supposed to be dead,' George shouted.

'Never trust an officer,' replied Walter.

'All right you lot. Over you go and remember, walk, don't run. That's an order,' bellowed Captain White.

Joe was first, followed by George and finally, a petrified Walter climbed the ladder to face the maelstrom.

Allied troops were being devastated by enemy fire because of the misconception that most German soldiers here had been eliminated by the seven-day barrage from the big guns or the seventeen mines that had just exploded under their trenches.

The Generals, particularly Haig, had underestimated how organised the Germans were. The Allies had not expected reinforced concrete dugouts that withstood fierce attacks. When the mines had finished exploding the Germans knew it was time to occupy their trenches. They simply carried their machine guns and positioned them ready to greet the British and their allies.

Walter saw George cut down by a shell explosion, bits and pieces flying everywhere. Keeping his head down Walter crawled across the muddy pockmarked ground, now littered with dead comrades. He fired many shots, but had no idea if any of his bullets found their mark.

He heard an order to fall back. He wasn't going to argue with a chance to save his life, crawling as fast as he could back to relative safety.

Looking around his trench for a familiar face, he didn't recognise anyone. Littering the space were dead soldiers who hadn't even made it over the tops of the trenches.

Walter was shaking like a leaf. An officer poured rum into the surviving soldiers' tin cups to calm them down. Walter gulped his. He'd never tasted alcohol before. He coughed and had another mouthful, enjoying the warmth of the brew.

The first day of the Somme would go down in the annals as the blackest in British military history – 20,000 killed and 35,000 wounded.

Walter and his platoon were given relief for a few days despite the battle raging on around them, and withdrew to the reserve line.

While Walter was in the reserve line he heard that his father's regiment London 5th were stationed nearby. He had not been informed his father had been reported missing presumed killed. Walter took the decision to leave the trench and walk the mile to where the 5th was positioned. It had been two years since he had seen his father and brothers and finding them was the very reason he enlisted in the first place. His decision was influenced by his undiagnosed condition of shell shock. He wanted to be with his dad and brothers.

When darkness swept over the valley he sneaked out of the trench and began his quest. As he walked along the dirt road, a motor vehicle approached flying a General's flag. The car pulled over and General Haig got out.

'Where do you think you're going, private?'

'Just enjoying the night air, sir.'

'What Battalion are you with?'

'The 19th, sir.'

'You're a long way from your post, private. Are you sure you're not deserting, running away from your fellow soldiers who have put their lives on the line?'

'No, sir, as I said, I'm simply taking a stroll.'

'I don't believe you. Hop into the front seat next to the driver. I'm taking you back to command headquarters.'

Walter did as instructed and the vehicle arrived at General Haig's headquarters at 10pm. After being locked in a cell with nothing but an iron bed and a bucket, he didn't sleep at all that night. His hands and legs began shaking uncontrollably. Around 9am an officer, Captain Hardwick, entered the cell and ordered Walter to follow him. They walked to an office where two other officers were seated.

'Private Jordan, are you aware just how much trouble you could be in?'

'Not really, sir, I was just going for a walk.'

'Were you? Was your commanding officer informed of your intentions?'

'No, sir, I didn't think it was necessary. I was only going for a short walk.'

'Soldier, you never leave your post whether in battle or not.'

'I won't do it again, sir.'

'No, you won't. Are you aware of the penalty for leaving your post without permission?'

'No, sir.'

'Death by firing squad.'

'Oh my God, no!' gasped Walter.

'So think hard about this question, private. Why did you leave your post without permission?'

Terrified, Walter explained how he'd hoped to find his father and brothers.

'What's your father's full name and rank and what battalion is he attached to?'

Walter gave the requested information to the officer who promptly left the room while the other two stayed with Walter.

An hour later, the major returned with a grim look on his face.

'Private Jordan, either everything you've told me is a lie or you're playing a very deadly game.'

'Sir, I've told you the truth, God's honour.'

Walter's shaking became even more prominent.

'I can find no record of a Sergeant William Jordan.'

'I don't understand.'

'Neither do I. Return him back to his cell, please, Corporal Hay.'

Two days later Walter faced a court-martial without legal representation. The court-martial found him guilty of desertion and sentenced him to death by firing squad the following day.

Walter was led to the holding cell to contemplate what was ahead. A sergeant entered the cell at 9pm and gave Walter a mug of rum, which he took gratefully. The sergeant returned several times with more rum throughout the night. By the time morning came, the sixteen-year-old boy was totally drunk and unable to walk without assistance.

Two soldiers arrived at 7am, bound Walter with a white cloth to restrain him before carrying him out to the courtyard where the execution would take place. They sat him down on a wooden chair as the same officer who had interrogated the young boy pinned a cloth over Walter's heart to provide a target for the firing squad.

Captain Hardwick ordered the firing squad to march into the courtyard and stand at attention. Once positioned, facing away from Walter, they would wait for the order to face the young boy and fire.

Although drunk with the rum that had been given to him by his sympathetic gaolers, Walter was terrified.

Captain Hardwick gave the order to face the condemned soldier.

Walter yelled out, 'Mother, Father.'

The officer ordered the squad to present arms, waited ten seconds and gave the order to fire.

Many of the shots hit the wall; deliberate misses; only two bullets wounded Walter. He was crying.

Hardwick unclipped his service revolver, walked over to Walter, and without a word, shot him in the temple.

The body was taken for burial at the local cemetery. Walter became one of the 306 British soldiers executed for desertion or cowardice during the war. Many of them were suffering from shell shock. His name would not appear on any memorial honouring the war dead.

TO CATCH A THIEF

CHAPTER 14

Lieutenant Colonel Oats had been informed by General Haig's office about Walter being executed for desertion but felt it would jeopardise the whole operation if he informed William at that stage.

William now had an idea why Captain Pittard had been killed but no solid proof. If he was to get a conviction, he had to catch these bastards red-handed.

Over the next few weeks, he put a plan together, which although dangerous, should uncover the truth.

Major Albright, the alleged gang leader, was, in fact, his commanding officer. William knew he would end up in a lot of trouble if he accused Albright of the murder and it proved to be a false allegation. He could even be shot.

William's plan entailed waiting for the next medical shipment to come into the store. He and five trusted soldiers would hide in six large packing crates with peepholes, allowing them to view the entire warehouse.

When the gang arrived to pilfer the drugs and replace the original manifests with the forged documents, they would spring out of the crates and arrest the perpetrators.

William arranged for each soldier to carry a Lee Enfield 303 plus one Lewis machine gun operated by the gunner in the end crate. He wasn't leaving anything to chance.

The storehouse was manned from 7am to 7pm, giving the gang a twelve-hour time frame to enter the store and steal the drugs. It also meant that William and his men might be stuck in their storage crates for a bloody long time.

Captain Sykes and his band of men entered the building soon after closing time and took a position in their individual crates. Each man had food rations and a water bottle; not exactly luxury, but it would keep them going for the duration.

Nobody could communicate with the others, so it was essential that each soldier knew the plan inside out. They couldn't leave their hiding spot, so relieving themselves was also confined to the crate.

At 3am, the large entrance doors were rolled open and an army truck reversed in. Two men were in the vehicle and two more walked beside it.

The gang approached the newly arrived medical supplies and prised open the tops with crowbars. Major Albright stood back, holding the two versions of the manifest; it was critical that the numbers were correct.

Once William saw them loading the supplies into the truck, he lifted the top of his crate, as did the other five soldiers. Pointing their weapons at the startled thieves, William shouted, 'Halt! Drop your weapons or we'll shoot.'

The gang knew they were outgunned and did as they were ordered. William approached his commanding officer and took the documentation he was holding, then handcuffed the major.

'I am arresting you all on suspicion of murder and stealing government goods.'

Sergeant Abbott, Corporal Bennet, and an unknown private were also handcuffed. William and his men arranged for transport to ferry the prisoners to the barracks for incarceration until a court-martial could be arranged.

William invited his team back to the cottage for a celebratory scotch. It had been a long night, albeit successful. After everyone departed, William tried to get a few hours' sleep before he contacted Lieutenant Colonel Oats with the good news.

'Hello sir, it's Captain Jordan.'

'You mean Captain Sykes don't you?'

'No sir. I've cracked the case. I think I should start going by my real name.'

'Cracked the case; good man.'

William went through the scenario and named the perpetrators.

Lieutenant Colonel Oats was astounded as he knew Major Albright very well, or so he thought.

A court-martial was arranged the following week with the four accused represented by a Major Thomas, barrister-at-law.

It didn't matter how good the defence was, it was a watertight case, with a guilty verdict pronounced and four death sentences.

The executions by firing squad took place in the same courtyard where young Walter Jordan had met his maker.

Shortly after the trial ended, William was notified of his son's death; to say he was devastated was an understatement.

Lieutenant Colonel Oats arranged three weeks' leave for William, Henry, and Sam to return to England and try to recover from their ordeal.

When William wrote to Victoria he had trouble finding the right words.

He simply wrote:

My darling Victoria,

I am alive and well and will be returning to England shortly to spend some time with you and the family.

Your loving husband

William

When Victoria learned of William's mission and the deception, she was furious but after a few days accepted it was one of the many sacrifices made during this terrible war.

William returned to the front as a captain, taking part in a number of battles including Passchendaele. He survived the war and returned to England and the police force.

Henry and Sam also survived the war, going home as corporals. Both joined the police force.

William committed himself to clear the name of his son Walter.

THE PACIFIC

YOU WOULDN'T WANT TO BE THERE

CHAPTER 15

Twin Falls is a small picturesque town in Idaho. Idaho is a state in the north-western region of the United States. It borders the state of Montana to the east and northeast, Wyoming to the east, Nevada and Utah to the south, and Washington and Oregon to the west.

Frank and Judy Robertson were third generation potato farmers. Their 2000-acre farm produced more than enough potatoes to keep the family very comfortable.

Robertson Family Home

Frank and Judy had two children John (21) and Beverley (18). John had recently graduated from the Naval Academy at Annapolis, Maryland. Bev decided to remain on the farm working with her mother and father.

John had been assigned to the 3rd Defence Battalion at Pearl Harbour. He was delighted that his first posting was in such a beautiful location.

That was until 7th December 1941.

John was the Ford Island duty officer and watched Privates First Class Frank Dudovick, James D. Young, and Private Paul O. Zeller USMCR the

Marine colour guard, march up and take their posts for Colours. Satisfied that all looked in order outside, John stepped back into his office to check if the assistant officer-of-the-day, Gerry Hudson, was ready to play the recording for sounding Colours on the loudspeaker. The sound of two heavy explosions however, sent the Marine officer running to the door. He reached it just in time to see a Japanese bomber fly past number 1010 Dock and release a torpedo. The torpedo struck the battleship *California*.

Hudson and John looked on in awe as wave after wave of Japanese planes strafed the harbour below them. Zeros and BSN torpedo-bombers were swarming over the harbour, dropping their lethal cargo. US ships were exploding and sinking quickly, their crews unable to escape the burning wreckage. So absorbed were they in the attack below, John and Gerry did not notice the two Zeros approaching from behind until it was too late. The Japanese fighter started firing; Gerry was riddled with Japanese bullets and died instantly. John received a leg wound and dropped to the ground, pretending to be dead. The Zeros passed over again very low - they were satisfied the two Navy officers had been eliminated. John squinted through one eye at the planes as they passed over. He could see the two pilots and the Rising Sun; there was no doubt who the enemy was. The Japanese attack lasted two hours and created absolute havoc.

Japanese Bombing at Pearl Harbour

American Losses:

4 battleships sunk
3 battleships damaged
1 battleship grounded
2 other ships sunk
3 cruisers damaged
3 destroyers damaged
3 other ships damaged
188 aircraft destroyed
159 aircraft damaged
2,402 killed
1,247 wounded

Japanese Losses

4 midget submarines sunk
1 midget submarine grounded
29 aircraft destroyed
64 killed
1 captured

John lay where he dropped until being discovered by a group of Marines looking for casualties.

They stretchered him down on a Jeep to the dock and transferred him to the Navy hospital ship the USS *Solace.*

The doctor examined the gunshot wounds and found three bullets had entered his left leg and another two in his right. John had been fortunate in that only one bullet had lodged in the leg. The others had passed right through, leaving a hole that could be cleaned and stitched.

Nevertheless the one remaining bullet would require surgery to remove it.

John was operated on the next day and was transferred to the Navy hospital at Pearl Harbour.

Navy Hospital

He recuperated for about three weeks reporting back for duty with a full medical clearance. He was itching to have a go at the Japanese.

Two days after Pearl Harbour, the Japanese attacked the Philippines. On Saturday, 14th February, the American defensive lines finally broke. General Macarthur and his battle-weary troops withdrew, declaring they would return.

By this time, the Japanese had captured Borneo, Celebes and Sarawak.

How was the United States going to halt the Japanese juggernaut?

John remained in Pearl Harbour as part of a defence force in case the Japanese decided to invade Hawaii.

He was transferred to the 3rd Battalion of 28th Marine Regiment in 1944.

Iwo Jima

Chapter 16

The Battle of Iwo Jima was an epic military campaign between U.S. Marines and the Imperial Army of Japan in early 1945. Located 750 miles off the coast of Japan, the island of Iwo Jima had three airfields that could serve as a staging facility for a potential invasion of mainland Japan. American forces invaded the island on February 19, 1945, and the ensuing Battle of Iwo Jima lasted for five weeks. In some of the bloodiest fighting of World War II, it's believed that all but 200 or so of the 21,000 Japanese forces on the island were killed, as were almost 7,000 Marines. But once the fighting was over, the strategic value of Iwo Jima was called into question.

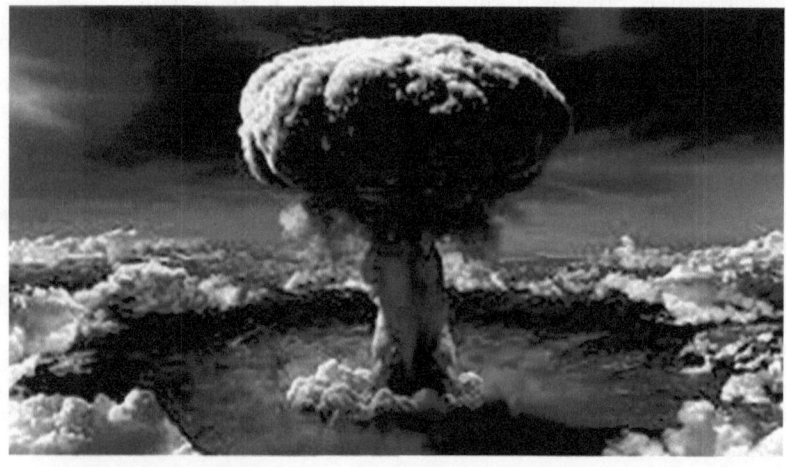

Captain John Robertson was part of the US invading force.

John watched as several battleships fired their big guns at the island. Iwo Jima could not be seen, but the shells were finding their targets. The warships also fired flares, turning night into day making the Japanese feel very exposed.

John decided he needed to get some sleep it was going to be a big day on the morrow.

February 19 1945

Captain Robertson and the rest of the Marines were woken at 4 am and given a hearty breakfast of ham and eggs and copious cups of coffee.

The invading force sighted Iwo Jima at 7am. The landmark was Mt Suribachi.

Mount Saribachi

The mountain was covered in defensive pillboxes, so the landing was not going to be a cakewalk. About 2500 yards from Mt Saribachi was another hill, also covered in pillboxes. Between the two was the beach where the American forces were to land.

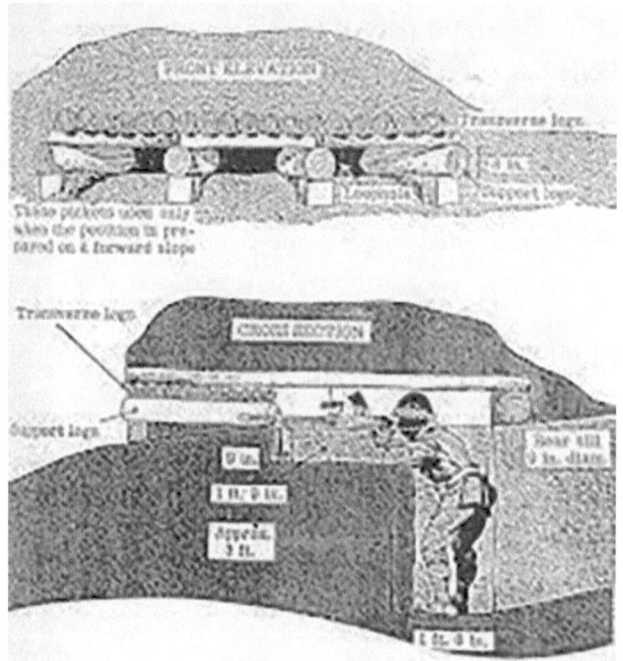

Japanese Pill Box

The American generals felt confident that the landing would be relatively easy. The Navy had been shelling the island for days and B29 bombers had dropped tons of bombs on the island. They were hopeful the Japanese had been softened up to the point where they would surrender within a short time.

Captain Robinson, and thirty-five of his men, were waiting in their landing craft (LCVP). Hundreds of similar vessels joined them in the first wave of the landing.

The marines encountered soft black volcanic sand, which buried their boots, making it difficult to make any headway. The enemy looked on, not engaging the invading enemy; not yet anyway.

Rather than engage the enemy on the beach, Lieutenant General Tadamichi established very strong defences inland using heavy machine guns and artillery.

Lieutenant General Tadamichi

He positioned his tanks to be camouflaged artillery positions.

The Japanese had been busy while waiting for the inevitable American invasion. They had dug 18 kilometres of tunnels, which were linked up to numerous command centres. These centres and barracks were up to 75 feet deep. The tunnel network allowed for troop movement to go undetected between defence points.

Captain Robinson commanded 100 marines, all of whom would follow their leader to the gates of hell if required.

'I think the generals have got it right. The bombardment seems to have killed most of the little bastards,' said Captain Robertson.

'Yeah, I think you're right, captain. Not much happening. We should be out of this Godforsaken island in a few days,' said Sergeant Wilcox.

The American forces were landing supplies and weapons such as tanks on the beach, unimpeded.

General Kuribayashi watched as the enemy landed troops and machinery on the black beach, confident their mission would be an easy one. After about an hour, he unleashed the full force of the Japanese fury on the American forces. The black sand turned red as it became a total bloodbath.

John kept his head down. Shells were exploding all around him, and he didn't think he would survive the onslaught. When it abated, he looked around to see if any of his men had been hit. Five lay lifeless on the black sand.

The *Nevada* and *Santa Fe* took out some of the Japanese positions with great accuracy.

Captain Robertson gathered his remaining troops and headed for their first objective, one of the three airfields in Iwo Jima. As they climbed the steep slope, he looked back to the beach. It was littered with bodies and overturned tanks. Other vehicles were bogged in the thick volcanic ash.

So much for a cakewalk, he thought.

The Americans carried on undeterred. Engineers blew up damaged equipment such as tanks and landing craft to ensure a clear pathway for the troops following. Despite the carnage 30,000 combat troops had landed on the island along with howitzers, which would provide artillery support.

By day's end, the Americans suffered 2,400 casualties, but it could have been a lot worse.

The infamous banzai charges the Japanese were known for did not occur as Kuribayashi did not employ this tactic. The Japanese would send out small units at night attacking American outposts. During the day, the enemy hunkered down and waited for the Yanks to enter designated killing zones.

Captain Robertson selected twelve of his finest to man an outpost under his control. It was a full moon, allowing for excellent night vision.

Their orders were to return by 8am. By 10am, Captain Robertson was concerned, so he took two of his men and made his way carefully to the outpost. What they discovered horrified them.

All twelve men had been beheaded. Their severed heads were placed on their chests. What made it even more macabre was that their penises had been severed and placed in their mouths.

John and the other two marines were physically ill. They did their best to dig graves, conscious the Japanese were ever present.

The three marines returned to their post, where none of them spoke of their grisly discovery. They reported that all twelve had been killed in action.

Captain Robertson was charged to lead his platoons, but he became withdrawn and unable to perform his duties as an officer. Finally, he was evacuated, and after a medical examination, he was sent back to America.

His diagnosis was "combat fatigue". Another 2,648 Iwo Jima veterans were also diagnosed.

After six months of treatment, he was given an honourable discharge. He returned to Idaho and worked on the potato farm until his death in 1965. He never married.

Iwo Jima was taken after 36 bloody days.

US Casualties 26,040

6821 killed

Japanese Casualties 18,375 killed

WELCOME TO VIETNAM

CHAPTER 17

Melbourne

Robert Hailes and Rick Jennings were great mates, who lived in the same street. They shared the same birthday, went to the same primary and high schools, and played football and cricket together in the same team. As they entered their mid-teens, they both met girlfriends. The four teenagers would frequent the popular dance venues, particularly *Opus* in South Yarra. It was at *Opus* that they first heard Billy Thorpe and the Aztecs play.

While Rob and Rick were dating Bev and Jan, Robert Menzies, Australia's Prime Minister, sent 30 military advisers to Vietnam.

That decision would shape Australia's future.

Rob and Rick's life continued on through the sixties. Both joined the Commonwealth Bank as trainee tellers in 1964.

The two friends turned 20 on 3 January 1965, and were obligated to register for National Service.

Their ballot took place on May 4, 1965.

'How are you feeling, mate?' asked Rob.

'To tell you the truth, one part of me is hoping I don't get called up. The other part of me wouldn't mind some adventure away from the bank,' said Rick.

'Yeah, I'm a bit the same.'

'Well, we'll soon know. They're just about to pick out the marbles.'

The numbers were broadcast on ABC radio, and Rick and Rob had their ears to the radio.

They heard their birthdate announced; January 3. They had been conscripted.

The two mates looked at each other and shrugged their shoulders.

'Oh well, at least we get an overseas trip out of it,' said Rob.

'Yeah, I suppose we do. I'm not looking forward to getting my hair cut short.'

The Birthday Lottery

The next conscript intake was July 1, so they had a few weeks with the girls before being shipped off for basic training.

They used their time having a good time with Bev and Jan. Both boys lost their virginity, convincing the girls that they might not come back, and that they deserved to die like real men.

Finally, July 1 arrived. Rob and Rick reported to Victoria Barracks, the Army Headquarters. Once they were processed, they were loaded on a bus to Puckapunyal Army Camp. Two hours later they were allocated their huts. This would be their home for the next eight weeks.

Registration at Army HQ

Both Rob and Rick completed their training without incident. They were sent to Vietnam in January 1966.

A BRIEF HISTORY OF THE VIETNAM WAR

The Vietnam War began in the 1950s through the conflict in Southeast Asia had its roots in the French colonial period of the 1800s. The United States, France, China, the Soviet Union, Cambodia, Laos and other countries such as Australia would, over time, become involved in the lengthy war. Finally, it ended in 1975 when North and South Vietnam were reunited as one country.

1887 – Vive La France

Napoleon III imposed a colonial system encompassing Vietnam and later Cambodia and Laos.

1923-1925

A young Vietnamese nationalist called Ho Chi Minh is invited by the Soviet Union to travel to Moscow and train as an agent of Comintern (Communist International)

February 1930

Ho Chi Minh founds the Indochinese Communist Party.

September 1940

Japanese troops invade French Indochina, occupying Vietnam. The French offer very little resistance.

Invading Japanese Forces

May 1941

Ho Chi Minh establishes the "League for the Independence of Vietnam" commonly known as the Viet Minh. Its purpose was to resist the French and Japanese occupation of Vietnam.

March 1945

The Japanese orchestrate a coup expelling the French and declaring Vietnam, Laos and Cambodia independent countries.

August 1945

Japan surrenders to the allies leaving Indochina in a precarious position. France once more exerts its authority over Vietnam.

September 1945

Ho Chi Minh establishes an independent North Vietnam.

July 1946

The French government offers Ho Chi Minh limited self-government. The offer is rejected. The guerrilla war against the French begins.

June 1949

Bao Dai, the last emperor of Vietnam, is appointed Vietnam's head of state by the French.

January 1950

China and the Soviet Union recognise the Democratic Republic of Vietnam. Both countries begin supplying their communist ally with both military and economic aid to support the resistance fighters. The Viet Minh ramp up their attacks against the French.

June 1950

The USA identifies the Viet Minh as a Communist threat. They provide assistance to France to combat the Communist insurgents.

March-May 1954

The French are soundly defeated at Dien Bien Phu, bringing about the end of French rule in Indochina.

April 1954

The US president Dwight D Eisenhower in a speech uses the term "domino theory" in relation to Southeast Asia.

July 1954

The Geneva Accords establishes North and South Vietnam divided at the 17th parallel. The accords also stipulated that elections would be held within two years to unify the country under a single democratic government. Elections were never held.

The South is led by a Catholic nationalist, Ngo Dinh Diem, while the North continues to be led by Ho Chi Minh.

May 1959

North Vietnamese build a supply route from the north into the south known as the Ho Chi Minh trail.

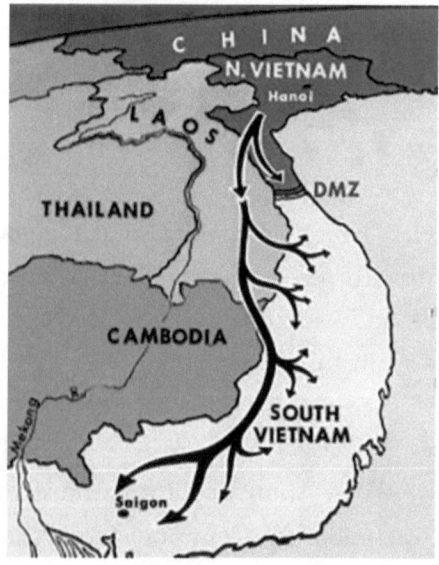

July 1959

A raid on U.S. soldier's living quarters near Saigon leaves several dead. The first American casualties of war

September 1960

Due to his ill health, Ho Chi Minh is replaced by Le Duan.
1961
President Kennedy dispatches 400 soldiers supported by helicopters to support the South Vietnamese war effort.

February 1962

Ngo Dinh Diem survives a bomb blast targeting the presidential palace. His nepotism to the Catholic minority was the motivation for the assailants.

May 1963

Ngo Dinh Diem orders his troops to open fire on a gathering of Buddhist protestors in Hue. Eight people, including children, are killed.

June 1963

A Buddhist monk immolates himself at a busy intersection, creating worldwide news coverage.

November 1963

The U.S. government realises Diem has to go. They back a military coup to expel him. He was brutally killed along with his brother.

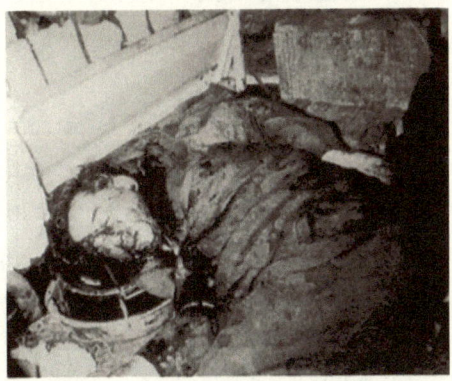

August 1964

North Vietnamese patrol boats in the Gulf of Tonkin attack the USS *Maddox*. President Johnson authorised air strikes on several North Vietnamese patrol boat bases. Two aircraft are shot down and Everett Alvarez Jr. becomes the first POW captured by the North. He remained their guest for over eight years.

Everett Alvarez Jr.

Congress passes the "Gulf of Tonkin Resolution" authorising the president to take "all necessary measures including the use of armed force" against any aggressor.

November 1964

The Soviets boost its military support to North Korea, dispatching aircraft, artillery, small arms, radar, defence systems, food and medical supplies. The Chinese send engineers to establish the North's defence infrastructure.

February 1965

President Johnson orders the bombing of strategic targets in North Vietnam in retaliation of Viet Cong raids on American targets.

Soon after, Johnson launches a three-year bombing campaign of targets in North Vietnam and the Ho Chi Minh Trail. The operation is named "Rolling Thunder". In March 1965 U.S. Marines land on beaches near Da Nang, South Vietnam. These were the first U.S. boots on the ground in Vietnam in significant numbers.

July 1965

President Johnson orders 50,000 additional ground troops to be sent to Vietnam.
The draft is now 35,000 a month.

November 1965

Protests against the war are becoming more prolific; Norman Morrison, a 31-year-old pacifist set himself alight in front of the Pentagon in protest against the war.

November 1965

In the first large scale battle known as the Battle of la Drang Valley, three hundred American troops are killed. In what became the American *modus operandi*, troops were both dropped in and withdrawn by helicopter.

U.S. troop numbers in Vietnam rise to 400,000.

June 1966

For the first time, American bombers hit Hanoi and Haiphong.
U.S. troop numbers stationed in Vietnam increase to 500,000.

April 1967

The protest movement was becoming stronger around the world.

Protest San Francisco

Protests in Australia were just as vigilant.

Protest in Melbourne Australia

London Protest March

September 1967

Nguyen Van Thieu wins the presidential election.

January 1968

The Tet Offensive begins, comprising a combined assault of Viet Minh and North Vietnamese armies. Attacks are carried out in more than 100 cities and outposts across South Vietnam, including Hue and Saigon, and the U.S. Embassy is invaded. The effective, bloody attacks shock U.S. officials and mark a turning point in the war and the beginning of a gradual U.S. withdrawal from the region.

February 11 – 17 1968

The worst week in the war for the Americans with 543 killed in battle.

February – March 1968

Battles of Hue and Saigon clear the Viet Cong from both cities.

March 16 1968

The Mai Lai massacre sees more than 500 civilians murdered by U.S. forces.

March 1968

President Johnson halts bombing in North Vietnam north of the 20th parallel. He announces he will not be seeking re-election.

November 1968

Richard Nixon is elected on a promise to end the draft.

September 1969

Ho Chi Minh dies of a heart attack in Hanoi.

December 1969

The U.S. government introduces the draft lottery despite Nixon's election promise.

1969-1972

Nixon gradually reduces the number of U.S. forces in Vietnam. The South Vietnamese were required to take more responsibility.
From a peak of 540,000 in 1969, there were 69,000 in 1972.

February 1970

Henry Kissinger begins secret peace negotiations with Le Duc Tho of the North Vietnamese government.

March 1969 – May 1970

The U.S. bomb neutral Cambodia, knowing the military action was illegal.

June 1970

Congress repeals the Gulf of Tonkin Resolution to control the president's ability to use force at his discretion.

January 1971

American and South Vietnamese forces invade Laos in an attempt to cut the Ho Chi Minh trail. The operation failed.

June 1971

The New York Times publishes the "Pentagon Papers", revealing the U.S. government had secretly increased involvement in the war.

December 1972

Richard Nixon authorises the most intensive air attack of the war in Operation Linebacker. The air attacks drop 20,000 tons of bombs over densely-populated regions.

January 22 1973

Former President Johnson dies in Texas at age 64.
The Selective Service announces the end to the draft and institutes an all-volunteer military.

January 27 1973

President Nixon signs the Paris Peace Accords ceasing U.S. involvement in the Vietnam War.

February – April 1973

North Vietnam returns 591 American prisoners of war in what is known as Operation Homecoming. John McCain was one of those released

August 1974

President Nixon resigns in the face of likely impeachment. Gerald Ford becomes President.

January 1975

President Ford rules out any further U.S. military involvement in Vietnam.

April 1975

Saigon falls to Communist forces the South Vietnam government surrenders. Helicopters transport over 1000 American civilians and 7000 South Vietnamese in a mass evacuation.

Evacuating Saigon

July 1975

Unification of North and South under communist rule becomes a reality.

By the end of the war, more than 58,000 Americans and 521 Australians lost their lives. Other countries that fought alongside the Americans and South Vietnamese were South Korea; 5000 killed, New Zealand; 37 killed, and Canada; 100 killed. Vietnam would later release estimates that 1.1 million North Vietnamese and Viet Cong fighters were killed, up to 250,000 South Vietnamese soldiers died and more than 2 million civilians were killed on both sides of the war.

2019

Vietnam is now a popular holiday destination.

VIEW TOURS

Rob and Rick flew to Saigon. They didn't have much time in the bustling city before they were flown out by helicopter to the Australian Army HQ at Nui Dat, right in the middle of Viet Cong country.

The two soldier mates began patrols soon after. They encountered Viet Cong fire several times, but remained unscathed.

Then came Long Tan.

August 18 1966
The Battle of Long Tan

The Battle of Long Tan in a rubber plantation in South Vietnam in 1966 could have been an Australian military disaster but is instead remembered as a decisive victory.

On August 18, 1966, D Company 6 RAR Battalion, consisting of 105 Australian, along with a three-man New Zealand artillery team, entered the Long Tan rubber plantations.

They had taken over from B Company in pursuit of enemy forces which a day earlier had attacked the Australian operations base at Nui Dat in Phuoc Tuy province.

About 3.30pm, a group of Viet Cong walked into the middle of the patrolling Australian soldiers who opened fire, wounding one and forcing the others to flee.

The Australian soldiers continued their advance, the three platoons of D Company - designated 10,11 and 12 - taking up positions around the rubber plantation.

Just after 4.00pm, the 28 men of 11 Platoon came under heavy fire from multiple directions, killing several soldiers and pinning them down.

As torrential rain began to pour, artillery support was called in from Nui Dat, as it became clear the Australians were facing forces better equipped and more numerous than expected.

Later intelligence showed they were facing a combined force of the Viet Cong 275th Regiment and the local D445 Provincial Mobile Battalion - between 1,500 and 2,500 soldiers.

10 Platoon attempted to rendezvous with their trapped colleagues - intercepting and killing a group of attackers before they too were attacked on three sides and their radio destroyed.

A radio operator braved enemy fire to restore communications and 10 Platoon was ordered to withdraw under cover of artillery fire.

Meanwhile, Vietnamese forces had advanced on 11 Platoon in a bid to negate the artillery support.

Artillery was walked closer to the pinned down troops, with shells falling less than 100 metres from the Australians.

Two 9 Squadron RAAF helicopters were called in to resupply the platoon and were forced to fly through torrential rain, with visibility close to zero, to drop crates of ammunition.

A resupplied 11 Platoon moved to withdraw, meeting up with parts of 12 Platoon who were engaged nearby, and eventually reforming with the rest of D Company.

The Australian forces were deployed in a defensive position as the enemy closed in, launching human wave assaults of infantry across the rubber plantation.

After several hours of intense fighting, reinforcements from B Company arrived on foot, along with A Company on board armoured personnel carriers dispatched from Nui Dat.

Three-and-a-half hours after the battle had started, the Vietnamese disengaged and the fighting stopped as quickly as it had begun.

Over the next two days, clean-up operations were carried out on the battlefield, rescuing the wounded and recovering the bodies of those killed.

Eighteen Australians were killed, including Rob Hailes. Twenty-one were wounded.

Two hundred and forty-five Vietnamese dead were found on the battlefield, with captured documents later suggesting hundreds more had been killed or wounded.

The Australian soldiers had been outnumbered 20 to 1 and despite their success against overwhelming odds, the Battle of Long Tan was still the costliest battle for Australia during the entire Vietnam War.

ABC News Report

Rick saw his best mate receive a volley of Viet Cong bullets to his face. He was unrecognisable. That vision would haunt him for the rest of his life.

Rick returned home to Melbourne without his best mate. He re-joined the bank and attempted to live a normal life. However, he began having nightmares, waking in the middle of the night in a cold sweat. Every time he heard a helicopter he would shake uncontrollably. If he was one cent out in his balance at the bank, he would suffer panic attacks and hide in a cubicle in the men's room. His relationship with Bev had ended on his return when she accused him of atrocities against the Vietnamese people.

When his annual holidays were due he decided to embark on a road trip to Adelaide to see his old army mate, Bruce Cook. He chose the coastal route as he had heard it was a beautiful drive, particularly from Torquay to Warrnambool.

He began his trip on Monday 16 April. He intended to attend the Dawn Service on the 25th in Adelaide, as he knew Bruce always frequented the service.

Rick hoped the trip would be a tonic for his depression.

He had passed through Lorne where he had stopped for lunch and was heading for the Twelve Apostles just past Apollo Bay. He intended to stay the night in Port Campbell.

12 Apostles

As he approached a bend in the road he kept going straight ahead, and the car fell fifty feet below landing on jagged rocks. Rick died instantly.

A passing tourist notified the police. They examined the crash scene, ruling it was death by suicide.

Rick's car at the bottom of the cliff

SUFFER LITTLE CHILDREN

CHAPTER 18

Post-Traumatic Stress Disorder (PTSD) has become endemic in some situations whether it is a sexually abused child to a refugee family fleeing a war torn country.

The medical profession works on a figure of about 25% of people developing PTSD after exposure to traumas such as a serious accident, physical or sexual assault, war or torture, or a natural disaster such as a bushfire or a flood.

Below is a list of examples:
6.4% of Australians aged 16-85 years
56% of Australia's Vietnam War veterans
31% of Australia's Gulf War veterans
7%-8% of people in the United States
30% of US Vietnam veterans
10% of US Desert Storm veterans
6-11% of US Afghanistan veterans
12-20% of US Iraq veterans
10%+ of US rape victims
3%-6% of US high school students
30%-60% of US children who have survived specific disasters
2% after a natural disaster (tornado)
28% after an episode of terrorism (mass shooting)
29% after a plane crash
100% of US children who witness a parental homicide or sexual assault
90% of sexually abused children
77% of children exposed to a school shooting
35% of urban youth exposed to community violence
50% of UK sexually abused children
45% of UK battered women

35% of UK adult rape victims

30% of UK veterans

18% of UK professional fire-fighters

13% of suburban police officers (Rates in urban police officers and officers in armed situations may be higher)

4-14% of US law enforcement officers

2–3% of the general UK community

16.5% of US fire-fighters

37% of Cambodian refugees

3% of Cambodian civilians

86% of women refugees in Kabul and Pakistan

10% in countries across the world (WHO)

20% after exposure to severe trauma and resource loss (WHO)

30-50% of a tsunami-affected population

32-60% of adult survivors and 26-95% of children survivors of earthquakes

75% of Bosnian refugee women

60% of US female rape survivors

15-35% of US patients with chronic pain also have PTSD

2% of US people who do not have chronic pain have PTSD

51% of patients with chronic low back pain had PTSD

50%+ of Armenian earthquake, mudslides in Mexico, Hurricane Andrew in the US

74% of a group of people seeking psychological damages following the crash of Pan Am Flight 103

16% of children and adolescents who lived approximately 100 miles from Oklahoma City reported significant PTSD symptoms related to the bombing two years after the bombing,

44% of Americans reported at least one symptom of PTSD after 9/11.

30% of those actually in the building or injured during the 9/11 New York City attacks.

Boko Haram

Boko Haram is a militant group in north-eastern Nigeria whose real name is actually 'Jama'at Ahl al-Sunna li al-Da'awat wa al-Jihad' which means Sunni Group for Preaching and Jihad. The group was founded in 2002, largely to preach an Islamist ideology based on the doctrines of the Taliban as well as groups such as al-Qaeda. It sought to disassociate itself from the Nigerian state and form a community only of its followers.

Wikipedia

Having virtually seceded from Nigeria, the leaders of Boko Haram knew that armed confrontation with the Nigerian Government was inevitable.

In 2009, the civil war began in earnest. During a major battle, Boko Haram's founder, Mohammed Yusuf, was captured and died in police custody. The group continued to target Christian communities in north-eastern Nigeria and traditional Muslim leaders who objected to the group's violent tactics or ideology of the new leader, Abubakar Shekau.

The Islamic warlord ascribes to a Takfirist ideology; he labels other people as infidels and believes this justifies the violent treatment of all others.

Abubakar Shekau

Izghe, Northern Nigeria 2013

Cricket was introduced to Nigeria by the British in the late 19th century and became a national sporting obsession.

Benjamin was playing cricket on the dirt street running through his village of Izghe. The boys playing with him were all about the same age, twelve. They couldn't manage two teams of eleven so they made do with six players a side.

His best friend Victor was bowling while Ben was wicket keeping, and they made a formidable pair. Benjamin's team won the game, which was as expected. There were no surprises in the result due to the fact that Ben, being the eldest, always picked the best players for his team.

When they finished the game, night was beginning to fall and the boys returned to their homes where the women of the household were preparing the evening meal.

Benjamin lived in a rudimentary shack with his mother, father, two younger brothers, Sam and Jacob, and his older sister, Rose. His grandmother also lived with the family group.

While the family sat around the table eating their tuwo masara, a traditional Nigerian cornflour dish, the conversation moved to discussing young Benjamin. His father, Joseph, announced that Ben would be spending some time with his brother's family in Maiduguri to learn the art of silversmithing, a highly respected profession. At first, Ben was not keen, since it meant time away from his family and friends. When his father explained how this profession would improve his quality of life, give him an income, and help support his family, Benjamin warmed to the idea.

The day came for Benjamin to move to Maiduguri. Many villagers came out to wave goodbye and wish him good luck. The saddest person was Victor. They had been born two days apart and had always been best friends. Benjamin too was sad to say farewell to his buddy.

The truck heading for Maiduguri was also carting cattle and produce to be sold at market. Benjamin crammed into the front seat with the driver and co-driver. The roads were not particularly good, making the trip uncomfortable.

Finally, they arrived in the city. Benjamin was amazed, for while there were fewer than 200 people in his village of Izghe, Maiduguri had a population of over half a million. There were people everywhere, plus cars and motorbikes zooming along the streets. This was all very foreign to the young lad having never even seen a motorbike before.

His uncle Emmanuel met him at the truck depot and took Ben home to meet the rest of the family. The house was constructed with mud bricks and had many rooms, nothing like the shack back in the village. Emmanuel showed Benjamin his room. Ben couldn't believe he would have his own room. Back home only his mother and father had a separate bedroom. Ben began to understand some of what his father had said about working hard. This was the direction that should be taken if he was going to enjoy a comfortable future.

The following day, Ben began his apprenticeship. The novice silversmith couldn't have predicted how his life would change forever.

Izghe

Victor was once again playing cricket in the dirt street of his village of Izghe. Although his love for the game hadn't diminished, it wasn't quite the same without Benjamin wicket keeping. The win-loss ratio had altered considerably now that Ben wasn't captaining the team.

The light was beginning to fade and the boys decided to end the match. They were picking up the fruit boxes they used as stumps when they heard the sound of trucks coming their way. The village didn't receive much traffic, so a convoy of trucks was an unusual event.

Six troop carriers rolled into the village. The boys, who had been enjoying their cricket game five minutes earlier, now stood by the side of the road watching in awe, bat and ball discarded on the ground.

Soldiers of Boko Haram alighted from the truck and began yelling orders to the villagers.

'Everybody come out of your houses and assemble in the street. All the men go to the far end of the village and await our orders. Women and children assemble at the opposite end. 'We are the liberators; we are Boko Haram. We are the protectors of the Prophet. You are Christians and don't deserve to live.'

The leader of the group approached the women and children, looking for boys he could recruit as soldiers and girls who would become sex slaves.

Next, the Boko Haram terrorists searched every house. Anybody they found hiding was murdered. Once the leader was convinced all the villagers were assembled, he ordered his troops to murder the men and any boys that weren't selected as recruits. The terrorists either shot them or hacked them to death.

Victor had two younger brothers; Charles, aged 7, and James, aged 5. They were killed along with the men, because the terrorists dismissed them as too young to be useful. Victor's grandmother hid under her bed, but she was found and hacked to death with a machete.

Victor was one of the boys selected. He was loaded into a truck and taken away to the Boko Haram camp over 150 kilometres away, hidden in dense bushland. His childhood of school, cricket and his belief in Jesus had just ended.

The trucks pulled up outside what looked like a jungle fort. Victor and the other boys were ordered to alight from the truck and were marched to a compound. This was also where the boys kidnapped before them were housed.

Over the coming weeks, the new boys were beaten and forced to attend executions, all in the name of Allah. They also attended classes conducted by the group's religious leader. If they were to become Boko Haram warriors, they must convert to Islam; if they refused they were killed.

Three months had passed since the time of their capture when Masud, the leader of the group, gathered the boys together, announced they were now officially Boko Haram soldiers and that it was time to fight the infidel.

Three trucks pulled up. The young warriors were ordered to climb aboard and their mentors, all seasoned terrorists, followed. Their objective was Sokoto, a village of three hundred Christians.

Victor and Comrades

The journey took three hours, and the trucks rolled into Sokoto at six in the evening.

'Everybody out, round up all the infidels into the village square. If anyone resists, shoot them,' shouted Masud.

128

The scene was bedlam. People were running away and being shot. Victor shot his first victim, the first of many.

Finally, the square was crowded with villagers and Boko Haram terrorists. Masud ordered the men and boys to be separated from the woman and girls. The soldiers then slaughtered the men and the boys they deemed not suitable for recruitment. They chose girls aged between 10 and 16 that would suit their purposes. They allowed the remaining women who were all too old to return to their houses.

Victor was proud of the way he conducted himself; a boy warrior.

Victor became a regular in Boko Haram, participating in regular raids and enjoying the raping of any young girls they captured. Any semblance of the young boy playing cricket and attending school was long gone.

Benjamin was sitting cross-legged in his uncle's workshop beating a silver pot into shape. Seemingly he had a natural aptitude for silversmithing and his progress had impressed his uncle Emmanuel who was giving Ben increasingly intricate pieces to work on.

It was near the end of the day, and Benjamin was looking forward to the evening meal. His auntie, Ruth, was an excellent cook, using ingredients from their garden as well as the odd goat or lamb from the small stock holding.

Ben left the workshop and walked the short distance to the house. Loud conversation and laughter could typically be heard emanating from the kitchen area where they all ate. Tonight there was only a deathly silence.

His auntie, uncle and two cousins were sitting at the table.

'Why the sad faces, everybody?'

'Sit down, Benjamin. I'm afraid we have some terrible news.'

Benjamin knew he didn't want to hear what was about to be said. He looked at his uncle.

Emmanuel disclosed the shocking news from Izghe. Now it was just his mother and himself left.

Benjamin quickly left the room and entered his bedroom, lying on the bed and crying uncontrollably for what seemed hours.

The family invited Benjamin's mother to come and stay with them rather than live alone with horrible memories. She finally accepted after some persuasion.

Benjamin worked the next day and although his mood was understandably sombre he was just as diligent as usual.

As the days passed into weeks and the weeks into months, Benjamin's auntie and uncle became more and more concerned about his mental state. Benjamin spent most of his free time in his room, not interacting with the rest of his family.

One morning, Benjamin didn't arrive at work as usual. Emmanuel waited an hour and then went home to see if Benjamin was unwell. Entering the boy's room, he found a note on the bed.

Dear Auntie Ruth and Uncle Emmanuel,

I am joining the JTF (The Civilian Joint Task Force).

I want to get the people who killed my family

Love

Benjamin

A similar letter was left for his mother.

Revenge

It didn't take Benjamin long to find the training base for the Civilian Joint Task Force (JTF).

Benjamin approached a soldier wearing the familiar light blue uniform of the JTF and requested information about enlisting in the civilian force. He was directed to a building at the far end of the parade ground.

Recruits Reading Oath of Allegiance

A captain of the JTF interviewed Benjamin. Once his story was told, the captain had no hesitation inviting Benjamin to join the people's militia.

After receiving basic training the young recruit was issued with the light blue uniform and an M16 semi-automatic rifle.

Benjamin was involved in a number of battles fighting Boko Haram, and he proved his worth as a soldier.

December 2014
Gumsuri, Northern Nigeria

It was a day like any other day in the small village of Gumsuri. Women were washing clothes, men were attending their vegetable gardens, and children were playing in the street.

The noise of trucks approaching alerted the villagers. They knew the reputation of Boko Haram and the devastation they would bring.

Then again, it could be the JTF searching for the terrorists, a much better alternative. Unfortunately for them, it was the former.

Six pickups drove into the village and about fifty Boko Haram militants disembarked and started rounding up all the women and children in one area and the men and boys in another.

Victor was part of the group guarding the men and boys. Once suitable recruits were selected, Victor and his comrades slaughtered the men where they stood.

The women and children were all bound and marched out of Gumsuri. The boys who had been spared were loaded onto the pickups and driven to the local Boko Haram camp.

It took two days for word to reach Maiduguri, as the communication tower in Gumsuri had been destroyed during the raid. A villager who had escaped brought the news of the massacre.

The JTF responded immediately, determined to free the kidnapped women and children. More than a hundred JTF soldiers, including Benjamin, set out in a convoy of trucks to hunt down the terrorists and bring them to justice. According to the JTF, justice for Boko Haram was a bullet to the head.

After travelling a hundred kilometres to Gumsuri, the convoy found only unspeakable horror. The civilian army group buried the dead and searched futilely for any survivors from the attack.

The group began tracking the guerrillas, a skill in which many of them were expert.

After three days, they came across the Boko Haram camp. Peering through the bush they could see women and girls contained in a large corral with a shed at one end.

Boko Haram soldiers were walking around or sitting in a circle smoking and laughing.

The JTF commanding officer, David James, signalled to his men to attack. One hundred JTF troops firing their weapons caught the rebels by surprise, and they were soon captured or shot. One hour later they had been defeated, and the kidnapped women and children released.

Benjamin scoured the camp, making sure there were no wounded. To his dismay, he discovered the body of Victor, his best friend. Benjamin fell to his knees and hugged the lifeless body.

Victor was only fourteen... just a boy.

When Benjamin returned to the JTF camp he became depressed. He spoke to no one unless an officer addressed him. He suffered recurring nightmares of the attack on Boko Haram where he dreamed he shot his friend Victor.

He was suffering typical PTSD symptoms.

He, along with sixty of his comrades, was called out to hunt down a Boko Haram group who had attacked another village. When the terrorist group was located, the order was given to attack. Benjamin ran screaming and firing his rifle without fear. He was gunned down in the first few minutes of the attack.

Benjamin committed suicide by Boko Haram.

ASSAD'S LEGACY

One death is a tragedy a million is a statistic

Joseph Stalin

CHAPTER 19

Bashar al-Assad

Bashar al-Assad was born on September 11 1965. That date in astrological terms means *"Progress, Adventure and Opportunity."*

Despite being the Syrian President's son he had no intention of entering politics. That was to be his eldest brother's fate. Unfortunately, Bassel el Assad was killed in a car accident in 1994. The pressure was now on Bashar to take over the reins at the appropriate time.

Bashar as a child was reserved, a quiet boy, unlike his outgoing older brother Bassel. Bashar lived in Bassel's shadow.

Bashar was a bright boy. He attended the Arab-French al Hurriya School in Damascus. It was here he learned to speak fluent English and French.

After graduation, he went onto study medicine at the University of Damascus, graduating in 1988. He specialised in ophthalmology and travelled to London where he joined the medical staff at the Western Eye Hospital.

The young graduate was living the life of a successful doctor in London, with wine, women and song. That all came to an abrupt end when Bassel was killed. Bashar was recalled to Damascus by his father to be groomed as his successor.

His initial training took place at the military academy at Homs in Damascus. Once he graduated, he was fast-tracked through the ranks to become a colonel in five years. He worked closely with his father, helping him to eliminate corruption in the government.

Hafez al-Assad, Bashar's father, died on June 10 2000. In Syria the law stipulated the minimum age to become president was forty. Parliament rushed through a new law changing the age to 34, which was Bashar's age.

A public referendum voted 97% in favour of Bashar to become President for a seven-year term. He was also voted to be the leader of the Ba'ath Party and commander in chief of the military.

The people of Syria hoped that having a young, well-educated President would bring much-needed change.

Syria's economy was a basket case when Bashar took over the reins. Russia no longer supported the regime as they were transitioning from communist rule. Much of Syria's oil revenue was squandered on the second rate military force.

The population had to be satisfied with mobile phones, satellite television and Internet cafes.

The economy did not improve. The corruption remained endemic and the public service continued to grow. Nothing much changed under Basher, including support for Hamas, Hezbollah and Islamic Jihad.

The people hoped that with Bashar al-Assad human rights would improve, but it was not to be the case. There were more travel bans against so-called dissidents than when his father was President.

He blocked Syrians from using Facebook and YouTube, and private messaging was prohibited.

Political opponents of Assad were tortured, imprisoned and killed. Like father like son.

Civil War

Following successful regime change in Tunisia, Egypt and Libya, protests began in Syria on January 26, 2011, demanding political reforms, a reinstatement of civil rights and an end to the state of emergency, which had been in place since 1963. Outraged by government inaction, the protests spread and became larger.

Protests in Damascus's Streets

When the government used deadly force to crush the dissent, protests demanding the president's resignation erupted nationwide.

The unrest spread and the crackdown intensified. Opposition supporters took up arms, first to defend themselves and later to rid their areas of security forces. Mr Assad vowed to crush what he called "foreign-backed terrorism".

The violence rapidly escalated and the country descended into civil war.

Assad used chemical weapons purchased from North Korea on his own people.

In total, over 5,000,000 people were killed with another 5,000,000 becoming refugees.

Refugee Camp Syria

Jamal was a five-year-old Syrian boy who lived in the city of Douma, located in Eastern Ghouta just fifteen kilometres from central Damascus. His three-year-old sister Aya and four-year-old brother Joram shared a rudimentary apartment with their father, Sayid, and mother, Maya Attar. Their aunt, Ousa and uncle, Houman Attar, lived in the next-door apartment along with seventeen-year-old Usma and his fifteen-year-old sister, Rasha.

April 2013

Eastern Ghouta became established as the centre for the anti-government forces, and therefore, a target for the Syrian government forces to attack. The Syrian government established a siege around Ghouta in April 2013, trapping 400,000 people in an area 100 square kilometres, making it one of the most densely populated urban areas in the world.

August 21

At 2 am, Sayid woke to the sounds of explosions nearby. He got out of bed and went down to the street below, where his wife and his brother and sister-in-law soon joined him.

'What do you think we should do, Houman? Do you think we should wake the children and flee?'

'Flee where, Sayid? We are imprisoned. There is nowhere to flee to.'

They heard a strange noise heading for them. It could only be a missile. All four ran for the apartment foyer, but they were not quick enough. The missile exploded, delivering its deadly sarin gas. The four adults from the

Attar family died from chemical poisoning. The five orphans would have to fend for themselves.

Panic in the Streets

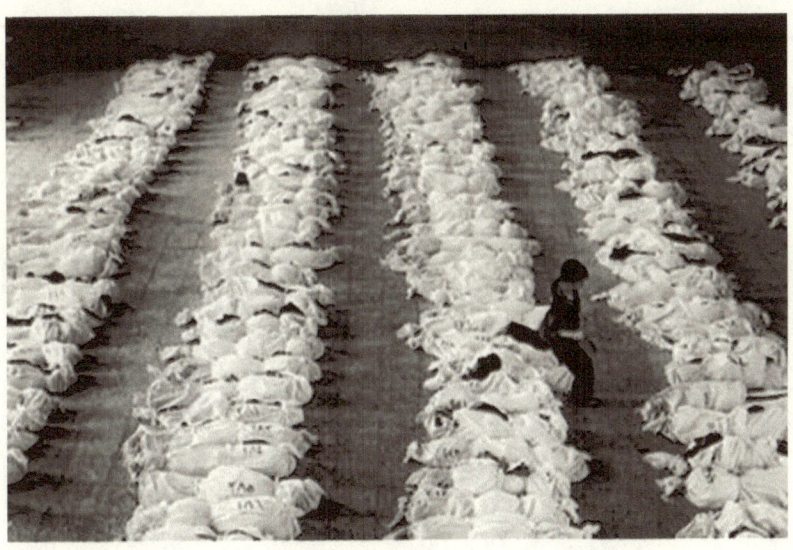

Approximately 1700 civilians were killed and another 3600 were injured.

The four bodies were wrapped in white cotton and placed in a temporary morgue ready to be buried the next day as dictated by Muslim law.

Once the Attar children buried their parents, they realised they were alone.

Young Jamal had not spoken at all since the attack. He just sat on the floor of the apartment, staring into space. The other children tried to communicate with him but they got no response.

Jalam(forefront) and his two brothers

Usama, being the eldest, became the patriarch of the two families he was supported by his sister, Rasha. Brother and sister would venture out into the war-torn city hoping to see a Red Crescent convoy distributing food. This was not a regular occurrence as Assad's troops regularly stopped the food entering the city.

Red Crescent Delivering Food

They were able to provide the family with one meal every two days; barely enough nourishment to stay alive.

Jamal remained silent. He never ventured outside, and when they heard explosions nearby, he would shake uncontrollably.

This poor little boy would suffer PTSD for the remainder of his short life.

Assad's children lived a much different life.

11 September 2001

It's just a date.
No it's not.

Chapter 20

It was a beautiful morning with not a cloud in the sky. The temperature was a mild 18 degrees.

John Bailey had just finished his shift as a Deputy Chief of the Manhattan Fire Brigade. There had not been any significant occurrences during his shift; only a couple of small fires.

He decided to call in to his favourite coffee shop, the *Coffee Bean*, and order a cappuccino and a French pastry.

He sat at the bar and as he began to drink his coffee, he glanced up at the television.

8.46

What he saw shocked him. A passenger plane had just ploughed into the North Tower of The World Trade Centre.

What a terrible accident! I've got to get down there and see if I can be of assistance, he thought.

John's brother, a financial adviser, quite often ran courses using the facilities of *Windows on the World*, a restaurant on the 106th and 107th floors of the North Tower.

He hoped to God Geoff wasn't running a seminar that day. As he ran towards the Trade Centre precinct he tried calling Geoff at his office.

'Good Morning this is Bailey Financial Services, Amy speaking. Can I help you?'

'Amy, it's John, Geoff's brother. Can I speak with him, please?'

'I'm sorry, John, he's not here at the moment. Can I leave a message for him when he returns?'

'Amy, this is very important. Can you tell me where Geoff is?'

'He's conducting a seminar at the World Trade Centre.'

'Oh my God.'

'What's wrong?'

'Turn on the TV in the boardroom. I'm sorry Amy, I've got to go.'

9.03

John was nearing the disaster site and he could clearly see the North Tower burning. He then saw a second American Airlines plane fly into the South Tower and explode.

This is no fucking accident. This is full-blown terrorism, he thought.

The first thing John did was to secure a set of powerful binoculars from a colleague on site. He knew it was a long shot, but he trained the lenses on the 107th floor where he knew his brother would be.

He saw Geoff standing on the window ledge. His beloved brother jumped.

Always the showman, Geoff swan-dived to meet his maker.

John was devastated, yet he knew he must help save the others trapped in the Twin Towers.

Deputy Chief John Bailey

After twenty-four hours, John went home exhausted, devastated and mourning for his younger brother. He at least had the support of a loving wife and his beautiful twin teenaged girls.

John had nightmares. Every night he would wake up in a cold sweat. The nightmare was always the same; his brother jumping from the 107th floor of the North Tower.

He became very irritable, not only to his family, but also to his workmates. He took to drinking heavily and smoking dope. He was offered counselling, but declined. After one year, his marriage had broken up and he had been fired from the Fire Brigade. He lived in a small apartment in the Bronx and socialised with no one.

John had a classic case of PTSD but refused help. He was walking down the Grand Concourse when he heard the familiar sound of fire trucks with their sirens wailing. The first truck sped by him. John stepped in front of the second. He was killed instantly. The driver received extensive counselling. He suffered PTSD for the remainder of his life.

Grand Concourse The Bronx

MALEVOLENT MARTIN

CHAPTER 21

A baby boy was born at Queen Alexandria Hospital on May 7, 1967. There seemed nothing unusual with that, as babies were born in Hobart, Australia, every day. His parents, Maurice and Carleen, were proud parents of their first-born son. Although young Martin spent most of his childhood at Lenah Valley, a middle-class suburb he also spent a significant amount of time at the family's holiday shack at Carnarvon Bay next to the Port Arthur Historic Site.

Martin was not an easy child to parent. Carleen often found his toys smashed on the floor. His overall behaviour was difficult. A psychologist's assessment was that he would never hold down a job. In one instance, he was accused of cutting down several exotic trees from a neighbour's block. Martin was suspended from New Town Primary School in 1977 for bullying other students and torturing animals. He returned to New Town Primary the following year. Although his behaviour improved, the teasing of younger children did not. He was transferred to a special education unit at New Town where he completed his so-called education.

The teenage years progressed with Bryant scoring an IQ of 66, a score bordering on a disability. Martin could neither read nor write and spent most of his time watching television with the odd bit of gardening thrown in.

Martin's parents encouraged their son to offer his services as a gardener and lawn mowing man. He enjoyed the work and social interaction very much.

In early 1987, while door-knocking in New Town promoting his gardening service, the 19-year-old Bryant met Helen Harvey, a 54-year-old heiress to a share in the Tattersall's fortune. Harvey was a lonely soul who had only her mother Hilza to talk to. The women shared the large run-down house.

Martin was befriended by Harvey and became a regular visitor, mowing lawns and assisting in feeding the 14 dogs who lived inside the house and the 40 cats living inside her garage.

Hilza died at the age of seventy-nine, leaving her fortune to Helen. Helen found Bryant infatuating, not in an intellectual way, but certainly in a physical way. Bryant moved into the Newmarket house. The couple enjoyed spending the Tattersall's fortune. They purchased more than thirty new cars over the first three years together. The unusual couple spent most days shopping in the Hobart CBD and eating in expensive restaurants.

The council made a ruling, prohibiting householders from keeping more than four animals at the house. Helen and Martin both loved their pets, so a decision was made to move to a 72-acre farm called *Taurus Ville* near Copping, a small rural community forty-five minutes' drive from Hobart.

It was in Copping where Bryant began his love of guns; firing an airgun at tourists and shooting the neighbourhood dogs if they dared to bark at him.

Bryant's life changed in October 1992 when Harvey was killed in a car accident. Bryant was inside the vehicle, but he survived, although he did spend several months in hospital with back injuries. Bryant was named the sole beneficiary of Harvey's will and he inherited a small fortune. His mother had the sense to apply for a guardianship order, placing Bryant's assets under the management of Public Trustees. The order was granted on evidence of Martin's diminished intellectual capacity.

By late 1995, Bryant had become an alcoholic and demonstrated suicidal tendencies.

He began to hatch his evil plan.

Martin Bryant 1996

Bryant being questioned by police

Martin Bryant 2019

145

Bryant boasted to his next-door neighbour that he would become famous not only in Australia but around the world. His desire for attention was overwhelming. His neighbour thought he was going to paddle to the Antarctic or something similarly stupid.

Martin Bryant was very close to his parents particularly his father, Maurice. Maurice had been very keen to purchase the *Seascape* B&B near Port Arthur for some time. Just when he felt he was close to having a suitable deposit, David and Noelene Martin purchased it. Maurice Bryant was devastated, and complained continually to his son that his lack of success in buying the B & B had ruined his life.

To Martin Bryant's simple mind, the Martins had deliberately purchased the property to hurt his family. Maurice committed suicide and that was enough for Bryant to seek revenge.

Seascape B&B

It was just before midday on April 28, 1996, when Martin Bryant pulled into *Seascape*.

In his car Bryant, 28, had packed two semi-automatic rifles, a 12-gauge shotgun, hundreds of ammunition rounds, handcuffs, rope, a hunting knife and tins of petrol.

Shortly after he arrived at the guesthouse, he murdered *Seascape*'s owners, David and Noelene Martin.

Bryant then travelled a few minutes down the road to the Port Arthur Historic Site, a former penal colony, which was bustling with tourists enjoying a pleasant autumn Sunday.

Broad Arrow Café murders

It was just after one o'clock and, lugging a heavy bag of guns and ammunition, Bryant walked from his old Volvo 244 to the *Broad Arrow Cafe.*

Bryant ordered a cheese and tomato toasted sandwich, which he ate on the outdoor terrace. Bryant then moved back into the café, and set up a video camera at a back table. He calmly withdrew a Colt semi-automatic rifle from his bag and began shooting everybody in the *Broad Arrow Café.* Within 15 seconds he had fired 17 rounds, killing 12 people and wounding 10. Bryant walked calmly to the gift shop where he fired 12 more times, killing 8 more people including the two volunteers working behind the counter. Two visitors were badly wounded.

Bryant reloaded his weapon and returned to the gift shop, searching an area he had ignored the first time. He found several people hiding in the corner. He walked up to them and shot Ronald Jary through the neck, then Peter Nash and Pauline Masters, killing all three. He didn't see Carolyn Nash, who was lying under her husband. Bryant then quickly moved to the gift shop counter, where he reloaded his rifle, leaving an empty magazine on the service counter, and left the building.

In the café and gift shop combined, he fired twenty-nine shots, killed twenty people, and wounded twelve more.

Car park murders

Bryant then moved towards the coaches in the monument's car park. One of the coach drivers, Royce Thompson, was shot in the back as he was moving along the passengers' side of a coach He fell to the ground and was able to crawl, then roll under the bus to safety, but later died of his wounds. Brigid Cook was trying to guide several people down between the buses and along the jetty area to cover. Bryant moved to the front of this bus and walked across to the next coach. People had quickly moved from this coach towards the back end, in an attempt to seek cover. As Bryant walked around it, he saw people scrambling to hide and shot at them. Brigid Cook was shot in the right thigh, causing the bone to fragment, the bullet lodging there. Fragments of Miss Cook's bone hit a coach driver, Ian McElwee. Both were able to escape and both survived.

At this stage Bryant had killed 26 people and injured 18. Six were slaughtered in the car park alone, with another six wounded.

Bryant Stalking in Car park

Tollbooth murders

Bryant returned to his car and exited the car park.

Witnesses say he was sounding the horn and waving as he drove.

The mass murderer drove along Jetty Road towards the tollbooth where many people were running away. Bryant passed by at least two people.

Ahead of him were Nanette Mikac and her children, Madeline, 3, and Alannah, 6.

The Mikac Family before the massacre

Nanette was carrying Madeline, and Alannah was running ahead. They had run approximately 600 metres from the car park, hoping to find a haven. Bryant opened his door and slowed down. Nanette moved towards the car, apparently thinking he was offering them help. Several people witnessed what happened from farther down the road. Someone recognised him as the gunman and yelled out, "It's him!"

Bryant stepped out of the car, put his hand on Nanette Mikac's shoulder and told her to get on her knees.

She did so, saying, "Please don't hurt my babies." Bryant shot her in the temple, killing her instantly. Next, he fired a shot at Madeline, which hit her in the shoulder, then shot her fatally through the chest. Bryant shot twice at Alannah, as she ran behind a tree, missing her both times. He then walked up, pressed the barrel of the gun into her neck and fired, killing her instantly.

Bryant drove up to the tollbooth, where there were several vehicles located. He blocked a 1980 BMW 7 Series owned by Mary Rose Nixon. Inside were Nixon, driver Russell James Pollard and passengers Helene and Robert Graham Salzmann. Bryant took out his rifle and shot Salzmann at point-blank range, killing him. Pollard emerged from the BMW lunging towards Bryant, who shot him in the chest, killing him. Bryant then moved to the BMW. He pulled Nixon and Helene Salzmann from the car and shot them dead, dragging their bodies onto the road and dumping them. Bryant then transferred ammunition, handcuffs, the AR-15 rifle and a fuel container to the BMW.

Bryant got into the BMW, leaving behind his Volvo, including his shotgun and hundreds of rounds of ammunition.

Bryant's toll was now 33 killed and injured 19.

Service station murder and abduction

Graham Sutherland, who had just been shot at in his car, reversed back up the road and drove to the service station close by, where he tried to inform people of the imminent danger. Bryant drove up to the service station and blocked a white Toyota Corolla that was attempting to exit onto the highway. Glenn Pears was driving, with his girlfriend, Zoe Hall, in the passenger seat. Bryant quickly exited the car with his rifle in hand and tried to pull Zoe from the car. Pears got out of the car and approached Bryant.

Bryant pointed the gun at Pears and pushed him backwards, eventually directing him into the now open boot of the BMW, locking Pears inside.

Bryant then moved back to the passenger side of the Corolla as Zoe attempted to climb over to the driver's seat. Bryant raised his rifle and fired three shots, killing her instantly.

Zoe Hall was the 34th victim killed.

Seascape roadway

Bryant opened fire on several vehicles approaching the entrance to the B&B but only wounded the drivers who managed to escape.

Martin then got back into the BMW and drove down the *Seascape* driveway to the house where the Martins, his first victims, lay dead.

Bryant removed Pears from the boot and handcuffed him to a stair rail within the house. At some point, he also set the BMW on fire. He is believed to have arrived at the house by about 2:00 p.m.

29 April 1996
Capture

Bryant was captured the following morning, when a fire started in the guesthouse, presumably set by Bryant.[1] Bryant taunted police to "come and get me," but the police, believing the hostage was already dead, decided that the fire would eventually bring Bryant out. Bryant eventually ran out of the house with his clothes on fire, suffering burns to his back and buttocks. He was arrested and taken to Royal Hobart Hospital for treatment.

It was believed that Glenn Pears had been shot during or before the standoff and had died before the fire. The remains of the Martins were also found.

One can only imagine what horrific images confronted the first responders to the Port Arthur massacre. Entering the *Broad Arrow Café* and adjoining gift shop they discovered 20 bloody bodies, many still sitting in their chairs with the lunch uneaten in front of them. Another 15 bodies were found outside in the grounds.

Many police, paramedics, nurses, and other first responders contracted PSTD and resigned from their careers soon after Port Arthur. Many who stayed on received very little support from their employers.

Port Arthur massacre gun law reform

A gun buyback and amnesty was initiated that allowed people to surrender newly banned weapons without legal consequences, with some people receiving payment funded by a Medicare levy as compensation. During the buyback, more than 700,000 firearms (both banned and legal) were surrendered to the police and destroyed.

Thank you John Howard and Tim Fisher for your tenacity in getting the new gun laws passed.

Scrapped Guns

ANYBODY CAN SUFFER

CHAPTER 22

Ariana Grande.

Ariana Grande

The Manchester Arena bombing was a suicide bombing attack in Manchester, United Kingdom on 22 May 2017. A radical Islamist detonated a shrapnel-laden homemade bomb as people were leaving the Manchester Arena following a concert by the American singer Ariana Grande.

Twenty-three people died, including the attacker, and 139 were wounded, more than half of them children. Several hundred more suffered psychological trauma. The bomber was Salman Ramadan Abedi, a 22-year-old local man of Libyan ancestry. After initial suspicions of a terrorist network, police later said they believed Abedi had largely acted alone but that others had been aware of his plans.

The incident was the deadliest terrorist attack and the first suicide bombing in the United Kingdom since the 7 July 2005 London bombings.

Ariana posted an image of her brain with PTSD and clear of PTSD to compare. The images went viral and made many people aware of Post-Traumatic Stress Disorder.

Whoopi Goldberg

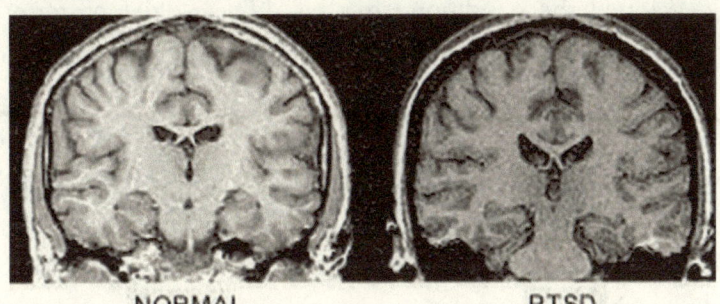

NORMAL   PTSD

Unsurprisingly, actress, talk show host, and comedienne Whoopi Goldberg spends a lot of her time jet-setting around the world for her work.

What you may not know is that each time she boards the plane she has a panic attack.

Forty years ago, in 1978, she was standing on a balcony in San Diego, enjoying the view, when she witnessed a plane crash mid-flight. Since then she has struggled to board flights.

Whoopi says, "If I see it, it lives in my brain." This is due to her being a visual person. Goldberg grew up in a deprived housing project and had learning disabilities.

Mick Jagger

Sir Mick Jagger is celebrated around the world for being the front man of the wildly successful band The Rolling Stones. Fame doesn't protect people from suffering from acute traumatic stress disorder or PTSD.

He developed the condition after his 49-year-old long-term partner L'Wren Scott took her own life. After one month of acute traumatic stress, a person can be diagnosed with PTSD.

Mick Jagger was reportedly "deeply upset" when his mental health condition was shared with the world. For the rest of us, it's good to see that nobody is immune to suffering the effects of PTSD. The band's insurance company paid out over $12 million after they cancelled concerts in Australia and New Zealand due to Jagger's PTSD.

Jacqueline Kennedy Onassis

Jacqueline Kennedy Onassis was the wife of President John F. Kennedy. Her world was turned upside down when she witnessed JFK's assassination.

She suffered in silence and little was known about her struggles, until Barbara Leaming wrote, *Jacqueline Bouvier Kennedy Onassis: The Untold Story,* which outlines the first lady's emotional struggles that were hidden behind a veil of glamour. Jackie suffered long term PTSD.

Monica Seles

By the age of 16, Monica Seles was a grand-slam winner and the world's Number 1 tennis player. Just a few months later, Monica was literally stabbed in the back with a nine-inch kitchen knife at the age of 19 during a court break at a match in Hamburg.

This event, combined with learning that her father had terminal cancer at around the same time, led to years of PTSD and an eating disorder.

Monica has learned to "live in the moment" and had a comeback before retiring from the sport. She worked through the loneliness and stress by herself and learned to love herself again.

Seles gained a lot of weight during the two years after her traumatic event, and she chronicled her battles with self-image in her book, *Getting a Grip: On My Body, My Mind, My Self.*

Barbra Streisand

Barbra Streisand is an Oscar winning star. However, her childhood was far from perfect. In addition to her father dying when she was just 15 months old, her mother failed to demonstrate any love. Her stepfather didn't particularly like her and showed her no affection.

Streisand developed anxiety while performing at a concert in New York when she forgot the lyrics to the song. As a perfectionist, this event affected Streisand quite profoundly.

She reportedly disclosed that she used anti-anxiety medication to get over her seasonally affective disorder (SAD) and anxiety disorder. Streisand is notoriously reclusive and doesn't like to leave the perfect order of her own home where she can control her environment.

Lady Gaga

Two years ago, the multiple Grammy Award winning performer Lady Gaga (Stefani Germanotta) opened up about her PTSD.

She suffers from PTSD due to being raped by an older man in her Catholic school at the age of 19.

Lady Gaga has opened up many times about how the trauma has long lasting effects where she relives the experience years after the event occurred. She gets therapy for PTSD and the symptoms, which were affecting her work commitments.

While collecting a patron award at the SAG-AFTRA Foundation's third annual Patron of the Artists Awards, Lady Gaga called the mental health epidemic a "crisis of epic proportions."

Tsunami.
Terror

Chapter 23

Hideaki, the captain and 50% owner of the *Kaza Maru*, was feeling very satisfied. He was returning to Kesennuma, his homeport, with a full hold of salmon. The captain and his crew of five had been at sea for over two weeks. They were all looking forward to being reunited with their families.

March 11

At 2:46pm, a 9-magnitude earthquake took place 231 miles northeast of Tokyo. The Pacific Tsunami Warning Centre issued a tsunami warning for the Pacific Ocean from Japan to the US. About an hour after the quake, waves up to 30 feet high hit the Japanese coast, sweeping away vehicles, causing buildings to collapse, and severing roads and highways.

The Japanese government declared a state of emergency for the nuclear power plant near Sendai, 180 miles from Tokyo. Sixty to seventy thousand people living nearby are ordered to evacuate to shelters.

The combined total of confirmed deaths and missing is more than 22,000 (nearly 20,000 deaths and 2,500 missing).

The *Kaza Maru's* crew had no warning. They were below deck sipping sake and singing their favourite songs. Their mood was determined by the knowledge they would be with their families within a few hours. Knowing also that their share of the salmon catch would be significant contributed to their happiness.

The boat rose quickly and began its deadly journey, travelling with the tsunami wave at close to 500 miles per hour. Surprisingly the *Kaza Maru* stayed largely intact and when it reached the shore it smashed through the levy and continued inland. Finally it came to rest. All aboard were killed.

Kaza Maru comes to rest

Tsunami damages Fukushima nuclear power station.

The earthquake and tsunami triggered the worst nuclear accident since Chernobyl. The Fukushima Daiichi nuclear power station located in the Pacific Ocean coast received huge damage from the earthquake and tsunami. The piping facility in the building, the facilities for the external power supply and backup power was destroyed. The next day, in early morning, the leakage of radioactive materials was found in front of the main gate of the nuclear power plant. The radioactive steam filled the reactor building as a result of the core melt down caused by the dysfunction of the cooling system.

Significant amounts of radioactive material was leaked into the surrounding environment through "vents" to reduce the internal pressure and the possibility of hydroponic explosions of the nuclear reactors.

According to estimates by TEPCO, the amount of radioactive materials released into the air was 770,000 tera Bq. It is said that this amount is about 20% of the Chernobyl accident. On April 12th, 2011, Nuclear and Industrial Safety Agency raised the rating of the accident from level 5 to the level 7, which was equivalent to Chernobyl.

As of February 2017, there were still about 150,000 evacuees who lost their homes; 50,000 of them were still living in temporary housing.

More than 120,000 buildings were destroyed, 278,000 were half-destroyed and 726,000 were partially destroyed. The direct financial damage from the disaster is estimated to be about US$199 billion dollars. The total economic cost could reach up to US$235 billion, the World Bank has estimated, making it the costliest natural disaster in world history.

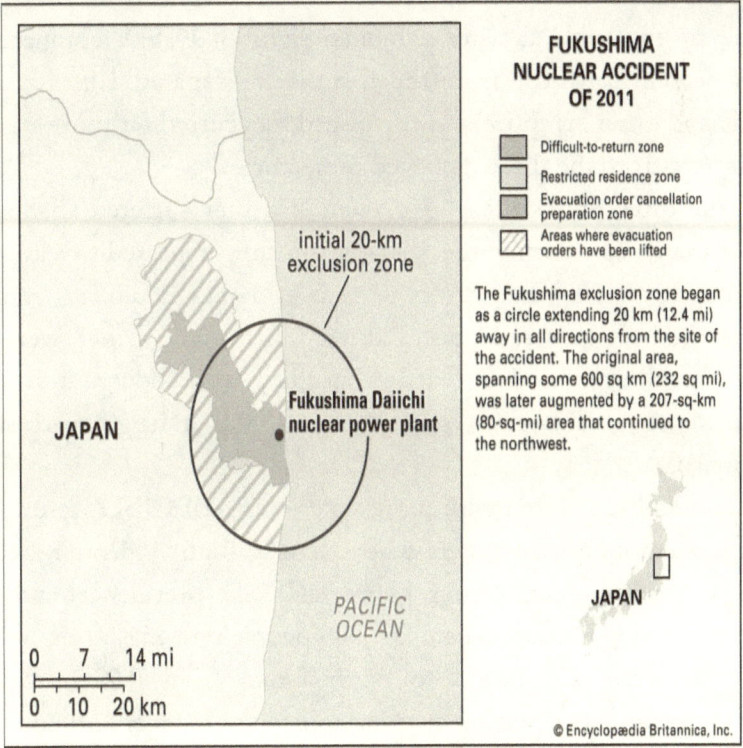

FUKUSHIMA NUCLEAR ACCIDENT OF 2011

Difficult-to-return zone

Restricted residence zone

Evacuation order cancellation preparation zone

Areas where evacuation orders have been lifted

The Fukushima exclusion zone began as a circle extending 20 km (12.4 mi) away in all directions from the site of the accident. The original area, spanning some 600 sq km (232 sq mi), was later augmented by a 207-sq-km (80-sq-mi) area that continued to the northwest.

initial 20-km exclusion zone

Fukushima Daiichi nuclear power plant

JAPAN

PACIFIC OCEAN

0   7   14 mi

0   10   20 km

JAPAN

© Encyclopædia Britannica, Inc.

On the three-year anniversary of the March 11, 2011 Great East Japan Earthquake and tsunami that annihilated the Tohoku coastline, a disturbing report from the national health ministry has revealed that more than 30 percent of children affected by the disaster are struggling with post-traumatic stress disorder (PTSD).

The new information echoes other recent reports of rampant depression and PTSD among survivors, many of whom have been barred from returning to homes deemed too close to the radiation-leaking Fukushima Daiichi nuclear power plant, alongside calls for better access to mental health care.

PTSD

Child psychiatrists interviewed 198 children from the hard-hit prefectures of Iwate, Miyagi and Fukushima – as well as 82 children from unaffected Mie prefecture. Parents of some of the children, ranging in age from 6 to 8, were also surveyed.

The results showed that 34 percent of the children from areas directly impacted by the triple disaster exhibited signs of PTSD, compared with only 3.7 percent for those from the area that was spared. Chronic anxiety, insomnia and other symptoms of the disorder occurred far more frequently in youngsters from the three damaged prefectures.

'In the three prefectures, 14 percent said they suffered flashbacks of painful experiences during the disaster or they repeatedly relived such experiences in dreams. Seventeen percent said they could not remember what they had experienced or stayed away from where they were at the time of the disaster and avoided what they were doing. Ten percent complained about suffering from insomnia and a heightened state of sensitivity.'

'Additionally, children with more severe cases of PTSD were found to express less emotion than others when viewing funny videos. Researchers also drew a strong connection between PTSD prevalence and life in temporary housing limbo – where 267,000 people remain.

Parents were also found to be suffering from PTSD, with their individual communities playing a strong role in the recovery process.'

'Of the 177 parents surveyed, 39 percent of those living in areas where residents are less friendly with one another showed symptoms of PTSD, compared with 23.2 percent for those living in areas where neighbours had tighter bonds.'

Important things to know about getting treatments for PTSD

- There are good resources and professionals to help you with PTSD
- You need a thorough check from a health professional before treatment is prescribed.
- Psychological therapies and medication are the most established ways to treat PTSD.
- New evidence shows that exercise and mindfulness are very useful for PTSD. They can be used together with physical and psychological treatments.
- Exercise helps other conditions that can occur with PTSD, like depression, anxiety, sleep problems, cardiovascular disease and obesity.
- You can get better. Many people who have had PTSD have been able to seek help, return to work, and live active, fulfilling lives.

There are three broad categories of treatment for PTSD:

- psychological treatments (talking therapies)
- physical treatments (medications)
- exercise, mindfulness and self-help.

Often, a combination of treatments works best.

Find the best treatment for you

Everybody has a different experience. Your symptoms, any co-conditions (like anxiety or depression), and your personal preferences will influence which treatments are best for you. Talk to your GP or mental health professional about the best treatment for you. Sometimes, a team will be involved in your care. It's still important that one professional coordinates and has overall responsibility for your treatment.

THE END

BIBLIOGRAPHY

Post-Traumatic Stress Disorder in Children   https://www.stanfordchildrens.org/en/topic/default?id

Stories of Syrian Refugees | Save the Children

Why is there a war in Syria? - BBC News

Civil uprising phase of the Syrian Civil War - Wikipedia

Bashar al-Assad - Facts, Father & Family - Biography

Syrian and Sephardic Surnames | SephardicGenJourneys

Do not forget the orphan children of Syria - The Lancet

The New Humanitarian | Understanding Eastern Ghouta in Syria

needs_assessment_fsl_eg_en.pdf

The Children Of Eastern Ghouta Are Living In Their Own Tombs | HuffPost

NYC Firefighters Share Memories From Ground Zero : NPR

Accounts From the North Tower - The New York Times

1st Hand Accounts | 11-September

The day before the storm: Photos of Sept 10, 2001 - 9/11 Remembered - Ten Years On - ABC News

Martin Bryant - Wikipedia

Port Arthur massacre (Australia) - Wikipedia

/ Martin Bryant - Wikipedia   https://en.wikipedia.org/wiki/Martin_Bryant

/ Port Arthur massacre (Australia) - Wikipedia

⌐ Hamilton Litestat Hartland Antique Brass Dimmer Switch, 1G 2W 400W | Fruugo

⌐ 7 Well-Known People With Post Traumatic Stress Disorder (PTSD)

▌ Post-Hurricane Stress, Anxiety, Recovery, and PTSD | Psychology Today

⌐ Japan Earthquake & Tsunami of 2011: Facts and Information | Live Science

⌐ High rates of PTSD and other mental health problems after great east Japan earthquake -- ScienceDaily

▌ PTSD Plagues Tohoku Three Years After March 11 Disaster | The Diplomat

⌐ GetFile.aspx

/ Category:Japanese masculine given names - Wikipedia

First published 2020 by Crabtree Pty Ltd

1000-Yard Stare is a work of fiction. Any resemblance to real persons, living or dead, is purely coincidental.

ISBN: 978-0-6484869-6-1 (p/b)

ISBN: 978-0-6484869-7-8 (ebook)

www.ingramcontent.com/pod-product-compliance
Lightning Source LLC
Chambersburg PA
CBHW030514260626
47157CB00005B/1743